Left Cross, Right Cross

G. CHIP GREENE

*Mary!
God's richest
Blessings!
Chip Greene*

ISBN 978-1-68197-502-3 (Paperback)
ISBN 978-1-68197-503-0 (Digital)

Christian Faith Publishing, Inc.
296 Chestnut Street
Meadville, PA 16335
www.christianfaithpublishing.com

Printed in the United States of America

Everyone must choose a cross. Whether you occupy the left cross or right cross depends on what you do with the center cross.

—G. Chip Greene, *Left Cross Right Cross*

Contents

Introduction

This story is about the life journeys of three contemporary lads many years ago. Jesus, Cris, and Daani will each draw their first breath on the same night in Bethlehem. Each lad will have examples to follow and choices to make. Each life will have a beginning and end with life's twists and turns in between.

They grow up together in Bethlehem as boys and go their separate ways as young men. The divine orchestration of providence will unite them once again at deaths' threshold. Jesus will occupy the center cross. One will choose the path to life eternal on the right side of Jesus. The other will choose the path to eternal damnation on the left side of Jesus. Come with me on this journey of discovery and choices. Come with me as we explore what might have been on the way to the hill called Calvary.

This is a fictional account. I made it up! Please do not look to this writing as historical or real. Remember this as you read. While I have strived to maintain the divinity and godhead that is our Savior Jesus Christ, there may be some questions. I am sorry if I have left something out or minimalized Jesus in any way. That is not my intent. He is my Savior first and foremost! I hope you are entertained and challenged as you explore these pages.

One Breath

As the evening waxed and the night air chased the heat of the day, a painful wail wafted out from the rocky chamber. A new breath was about to be taken, and the young mother pushed with all her might to accomplish delivery.

Soon, the cries of childbirth give way to tears of joy that mingle with the sound of infant cries. The infant, no longer confined to mothers' womb, is unsure and lets all those gathered 'round know his contempt for this new world. This baby boy, already named before birth, has the expectations of all mankind resting on his tiny shoulders.

Jesus, son of the Most High, nevertheless, born to a simple young woman of faith and an unsure earthly father. The Christ child, foretold since the beginning of time, finally comes to earth veiled in human flesh.

He is meant to live, breathe, and die like all mortal men, yet unlike any who had ever been or would ever come. He is meant to experience all this world has to offer but remain untouched by mortal desires and failure, meant to influence and affect all he touches, meant to change the world and offer hope to all who accept his teaching. And ultimately, he is meant to affect all of eternity.

It is such a tall order for such a tiny baby. And so this scene, varied in its exactness, is played out in two other modest dwellings in the nearby village. Each struggle and pain in child birth is met with relief of the delivered baby boy.

Three brand new lives. Three possibilities of getting it right. Three miracles set in motion by unseen direction, each with a purpose established before the beginning of time.

Two Dreams

As Naomi stared in wonder at the new life she had just delivered, her joy and gladness quickly remembers the stark circumstances of her existence. She glances from her new baby boy for a second and takes in the darkness just outside the pale light the single candle flicker casts.

All alone, save for the baby. She remembers the grim prospects for survival that awaits her beyond the safety of the light. Now, beyond all belief, she has accomplished the birth of this—her son, a dark secret finally given breath.

She sighs and holds her newborn close. A tear forms in her eye and cascades quickly, running down her cheek, landing on the now still form of the child.

Naomi knows it won't be long until her presence is discovered in the back room of the vacant building come first light.

The discovery will chase her from shelter into the streets and back lots once again.

This time will be different, though. Naomi will have another life to care for and protect. Another, she soon realizes, that she would protect with her very being. As Naomi drifts into the enormity of what lays ahead for her and the child, she realizes a simpler task needs to be completed and sets her mind to that.

"What shall you be called?" Naomi whispers to the suckling child. "I must give you a name. A name that will set you apart."

She pauses to think and then softly says, "Daani, this shall be your name. Everyone that hears it will know who you are."

Content that she has done enough for the present and suddenly not caring about what lay ahead, Naomi closes her eyes for much needed rest, no longer alone.

Across the street and a few dwellings down, a much different birth event has just taken place. This birth has many participants and is filled with great anticipation and longing. A planned event, in as much as you can plan the natural process of childbirth. The humble dwelling is filled with many family members separated by rooms. Those involved with merriment and excited expectation are corralled in the main section of the home. Those that would be seconds in the childbirth process are gathered with the mother to-be and share every painful breath and muscle contraction until their fruition.

The final push and first breath and cry of the baby boy are greeted from both rooms with hugs and tears of joy. The long antici- pated fulfillment of the young parents' love and commitment to each other has voice. Just as it should be, perfect in every detail.

The midwives hustle and care for mother and child. The young father is ushered in to see his newborn son. His brash and puffed-up ego quickly soften as he sees for the first time his heir, his namesake.

Leaning close to give his exhausted wife a kiss and touch the cheek of his first child, he knows this is a moment like no other in his short life, set in motion by God Himself. This is a moment of great responsibility and a moment where he entrusts the son to the mother.

Wise to recognize the bond of mother and child as holy, he softly addresses his wife. "Ellise, you have done well and have blessed me beyond measure. By what name shall we call our son?"

Ellise responds quickly, as she had already spent countless hours thinking of this very moment, "We shall call him Cris, and he shall be known by all that hear his name."

Three families, uniquely different in earthly circumstances yet all destined to be intertwined for eternity. God's plan for all mankind will inexplicably be shaped by the play and interaction of these boys.

Three Lives

One

Mary is not any different than all young mothers. She wants only the best for her son and is always protective. Mary knows in her very soul that Jesus is special. Blessed and protected by God, Jesus's first years quickly go by. Filled with lessons and learning at the side of Mary and the other women in the neighborhood, Jesus quickly learns safety at the knee of his mother. No matter what task she is undertaking Mary always has time for shepherding her son.

Mary often has the feeling that the entire world revolves around her son and his growth.

Always provided for by her often absent husband Joseph, Mary never wants for shelter, food, or love. Truly, she is blessed among women.

Joseph is away from his family for many days at a time as his skill as a stone mason is highly esteemed, and the labor comes easy for him.

As a young father, Joseph cherishes the time he spends with his God-given son. Father and son spend many evenings together, each wondering at the other's accomplishments of the day and the plans for tomorrow. Every time Joseph holds his son, he feels God and His presence.

Yet there is an uncertainty that he cannot explain when it comes to Jesus and his future. Joseph just knows that Jesus will have a greater calling than his own. It seems every time he looks Jesus in the eyes, he sees something deep and inexplicable.

It was a perception he has never felt before. He doesn't fully understand why he feels this way, but he just knows there is something more about this boy, more to be revealed, more to come.

Jesus too has a curious longing. What lay beyond the safety of his home territory?

As he grows in stature and knowledge, he cannot contain the thoughts about his surroundings. At Mary's side, he presses for details of what is beyond their eyesight, and the source of unknown noises fills his heart with wonder. The noises coming from the surrounding homes and streets beckoned to him daily.

And then one day, at the age of seven, Jesus can't take it any longer. He finds himself safely away from the mom's gathering and able to round a corner and is out of sight.

Two

Naomi finds her life wonderfully complicated by the presence of her son Daani. She has never had an easy existence, but she has never before had a reason for hope either. She finds something special every time she looks into the face of her child.

Naomi sees a promise, a promise that is yet to be realized or imagined. This insight seems to soften the reality of their situation. The early years for the two of them proved that living from day to day was possible, but certainly not easy. The bond of two humans who count so much on each other strengthen with every moment.

Daani masters the streets at an early age and is adept at being seen and not seen in the blink of an eye. Scrounging and gleaning became a necessity as much as a challenge in their survival. Mother and son count on each other in ways the surrounding families cannot imagine.

Daani is as much at home away from Naomi's side as beside her. Naomi trusts something or someone far greater than herself to alleviate her fears every time Daani is out of her eyesight. There is a certain peace in her heart, a feeling that Daani is to be a part of a greater purpose here on earth.

And so it was that one day, a day like many others in the past, Daani stole away from his mother's side. This time, however, he knew the day would hold something very special, a gift.

Three

Ellise sighs as she sits beneath the shade of her home's willow tree. This tree sprouted from under the few stones that lay flat as a walkway between the houses and provides much welcome shade during the heat of the midday sun. Its growth is a source of joy in the sun-parched land.

Cris has his own agenda for the day, as he often did. So independent and sure of himself, he never seems to wait for anything or anyone. He certainly never looks to his mother for confirmation of his actions or plans for the day.

Ellise has been blessed with two more children since Cris's birth seven years before, and her days are, needless to say, full of containing the crisis at the moment and planning for the probability of one later.

Cris often found it easy to go unnoticed for great lengths of time. It was not that Ellise no longer cared for her growing son; it's just that Ellise was compelled by much more near and urgent cries. Besides, Cris was a big boy now and was filling out quickly.

As Cris silently slips away from the sound of everyday life at his house, he plots in his mind a course of action for the day. Unaware that a much larger plan has already been set in motion, Cris heads to one of his favorite hiding spots.

And so it is on that day long ago the hand of God begins to entwine the lives of three young boys. Each life stamped with the seal of eternity and destined to be written in the archives of immortality.

Into the Unknown

Jesus carefully picks his way along the unfamiliar passages, often glancing back to see if he is being followed. Right now, he doesn't care about anything but finding out what lay around the next corner or what is under the next overhang.

Soon, he finds himself completely removed from anything looking familiar and facing a curious opening between two buildings. As he peers into the opening, he can see that there is a short passage, and he can see light on the other side. The opening and passage seem somehow friendly and beckon to him. He enters in.

The pass is just small enough that he has to stoop his young frame to stride the six or seven feet through and into the opening. Jesus stands as he enters and notices movement further back and into a shaded area. Surprised to think that another is in this space too, Jesus calls softly, "Hi, anybody here?"

No sooner has the words left his mouth that another boyish shape appears from the spot and shields his eyes as he enters the same sunlit space that Jesus occupies.

"Hi yourself," Cris says. "What are you doing in here?"

Jesus senses that he has somehow transgressed on sacred ground and quickly answers, "I'm Jesus and didn't mean to scare you."

Cris replies, "Scare me? Nah, I was just kinda surprised to see you here."

Then like most seven-year-olds when not under the stifling glare of a parent, they sit down in the sun and make friends. They quickly find out all the essential things any boy would require knowing about a new friend and were engrossed in sharing when Jesus looks over the shoulder of Cris and sees another childlike figure move silently through the passage and into the opening.

As they soon find out, this youngster named Daani has stumbled innocently enough into the same space already occupied by Jesus and Cris. After the requisite feeling out and inquiries, Daani too soon settles comfortably into the growing circle of newfound friends.

Daani offers new food to the conversation, and the boys soon learned how much they have in common and how much they have to learn about each other.

A bond is quickly struck, and Daani pipes in, saying, "This is our very own spot. Nobody else better find out 'bout this. We have to promise not to tell anybody where it is."

Jesus, Daani, and Cris all agree that indeed this is the beginning of something special and secret. Jesus is in agreement with his new friends and already knows what he will say when Mary asks where he has been for so long. Daani and Cris too have thought about how "much" they will tell their moms.

As the sinking sun begins to cast long shadows in the hide, the boys all come to the same conclusion: they need to get home now. All three boys backtrack safely to their homes, and although the respective mothers were upset that they had been away without permission, they were happy that each had found new friends.

Mary was the first to probe the mind of her young adventurer and simply asks, "How far did you wander today?"

Jesus somehow knows that his mother won't appreciate all the explorations he experienced. So he describes the two other boys he met and some of the things they talked about. He did mention the neat spot they had discovered too, knowing full well he could trust his mother.

Jesus knows his dad will be a much better sounding board for what he discovered today and decides to save the other details for later, during a quiet time with Joseph. And besides, he suddenly was worn out and realized that he had put his growing mind and body through a lot for one day. He has so very much to think about and take in, and sleeping always seems to calm his spirit and renew his mind.

Jesus was sure that Mary was still talking, and he was still waiting for his dad to come home when he drifted off to sleep with his head on Mary's lap. The last thing he remembers is the comforting smell of his mother and the warmth of his home.

Ellise barely noticed when Cris slips into the house. She smiles to herself to see him safely back but was just as happy to know that her house was quiet, and there was no demand for her attention. She lets Cris silently glide to his room without saying a word.

As Daani sought Naomi and their eyes meet, she has that look on her face. The motherly look suggests she is just glad that his adventures of the day had come full circle and they were once again together.

Naomi clutches Daani as he sits down next to her, taking a physical inventory of her son as he settles. Assured that he was no worse for the days traipsing, Naomi begins slowly rocking and humming, holding tight her most prized possession.

They gaze into the clear night sky and instinctively pull tattered covering up to their chins, sure they will need it all to brave the cool night together.

Divine Purpose

Only in the Father's perfect time does He determine what is known and what is to be known. And so it is even with the Son of Man.

It was one of those quiet mornings that Jesus finally begins putting together the reason for his sound sleep. He was always curious how he began each day with more knowledge of his heavenly purpose. As long as he didn't think about it too much, it made some kind of sense to him. He was able to connect with something much larger than himself during this slumber time.

It is at this young age that he consciously makes the connection. His Father spoke with him nightly and was instilling in him the knowledge of the universe and mankind. It is strange to Jesus as even in this human form, he remembers the beginning of all time and space. Indeed, it is like a dream.

So with newfound understanding, Jesus looks forward to his time of rest and sleep. He dares not mention this discovery to his parents as he is pretty sure it isn't the proper time or place yet.

Anyway, he senses he has plenty of time to reflect on his God side, and right now, his human side is imploring him to build on his boyhood relationships and growing up.

Sons of Israel

Jesus's head is covered with curly brown hair that hangs to his shoulders. His soft gray eyes seem to offer a window through which you can glimpse his soul. His slight build is typical of a lad his age and does not suggest any predisposition of carrying the hopes and promises of the entire world upon them. His feet are already calloused in all the right spots to aid him in running and jumping and have worn nicely into the handmade leather sandals he regularly wears around the house and outside.

His clothing is fashioned lovingly by Mary and hangs loosely around his frame with thought of many months of wear as he grows. Though coarse in its weaving, Mary has spent many hours making it and kneading the cloth with her loving hands to soften the fabric for her son.

Jesus loves the times he has a restful spirit, and he sits and watches his mother while she works around their home. Mary moved with a graceful purpose and always seems busy but not overwhelmed. She seemed to love being in command of the surroundings and cherished every moment of home life. Jesus is pretty sure she is an angel sent to protect and nurture him as he grows.

Cris has dark, almost black hair that Ellise always keeps trimmed to his earlobes. Straight, with not a curl in sight, Ellise liked the neat look that this presented and never bothered to ask Cris what he thought. Cris didn't care anyway as he just enjoyed the time his mom spent touching his hair when she trimmed and fixed it.

Cris has grown fast and has already begun to lose the boyish shape in both his body and face. His dark-brown eyes and heavy eyebrows always seem to make him look more serious than he is. This leads others to think he is older than the boys his own age.

He tends to carry himself with his shoulders back and his chin out, and this contributes to his mature demeanor too. Cris's clothes are made by others, and Ellise takes great pride in that fact. She always adorns the clothes with colored beads and thread and other highlights to make them stand out even more, adding a mother's touch.

Ellise is a part of a large well-liked family that has been in the village for many years and generations. Traditional in every sense, the grandparents and aunts and uncles figure prominently in every decision that is made by the family. The presence of so many people living in one household, however, has an adverse effect on Cris as he often finds himself left out and on the outside.

Cris often feels as if he is left to figure a thing out for himself. And consequently, that is what Cris becomes good at doing, even at a young age.

Daani brushes his wavy cinnamon-colored hair aside as he stretches to pull his tattered shirt over his head. His thin frame is deeply chiseled and without an ounce of fat anywhere. His light-brown eyes are soft to look at yet steely in their perception of the world around them. Daani's complexion is as smooth as silk and his skin tans easily as he roams about. The years of living with his mother on the street and fending for themselves has already shaped him into a wise and cunning lad, with discernment a trademark.

Naomi had to trust Daani and his judgment at a very young age, and she could see the confident young lad blooming, even in these harsh conditions. Oh, how she loves this boy, her only son, and wishes every day their lives could be better.

Relationships

The relationship of the three boys is special to say the least. How lucky they were, thinking they had so much in common. As only friends can do, they look past the obvious differences of families, homes, and status and went to common ground, the only thing that made sense to them. Their relationship as friends and cohorts revolved solely around what they had in common.

Their world could go to pieces around them, and they would always have each other. That was never more evident than the day Daani showed up at the hide late. Daani was always the first one to the hide on the days they got together. It was so unusual that Cris and Jesus had already planned out a couple of adventures for the day.

Cris looked up when Daani came in and said, "Where you been? Half the day is already gone!" Jesus quickly grabs Cris's arm as if to say, *Lay off!* Jesus walks over to Daani and puts his hand on his shoulder. Jesus just stands there without saying a word. Daani finally looks up, and Jesus can see right away there is anguish on his face, written in his eyes. There is nothing in their young lives that could have prepared them for what Daani is about to relate.

Hidden Glory

The boys fall to the ground in unison as the tears begin to fall freely from their cheeks. Jesus and Cris cannot believe what Daani has just revealed! Daani's mom, Naomi, has died in the night.

Daani relates that as the new day cast light and warmth upon their sleeping spot, he had stirred and nudged his mom in the process. This was their usual way to wake each other in the morning. When Daani did not get the expected response, he repeated the process with the same result—nothing. It took a few moments for Daani to realize that something was wrong, and he uncovered Naomi's face. He brushed back her flaxen hair. He knew at that moment his mother was gone.

As he stroked her cheek, he noticed she still had warmth emanating from her skin. He could not help but see how peaceful she looked, as if her cares were now separated from her body forever. As the enormity of this discovery began to sink in, Daani fell to his knees and softly laid his head in her lap. He knew his life was about to change. He had no idea what that truly meant.

His sorrow cried for an end, and he lost himself in fitful sleep. When Daani finally was able to wake from the terrible dream he had, he couldn't wait to share it with Naomi. Once again, as he had done many times before, he nudged her, but he received no response.

The truth shot through his soul like a lightning bolt. He lifted his numb body and stumbled into the morning light. His only hope lay in the comfort he knew would come from making it to the hide and his brothers.

The three friends have never seen each other cry and all the emotion that is contained within it. They have no idea what this event will mean to all of them. As the initial shock wears off, the boys regain the ability to speak. Their thoughts turn to Daani and what he wants, needs, and thinks.

They know they have to go with him back to where Naomi is. They are terrified! Jesus and Cris know they have to do this for Daani. Daani knows he has to be sure that this is not really some kind of nightmare So with Daani leading the way, they head to where Naomi lays. It seems like it takes forever to reach the spot where mother and son had spent the night.

Jesus has no idea what they will do when they got there. Cris knows this is something that he will remember for the rest of his life, and Daani dreads seeing the still form of his mother once again and begins to weep.

As they approach the bundle of rags that holds Naomi, Jesus motions to Cris and Daani to stop. He speaks softly saying, "Let me go first and see for myself."

As Jesus steps off the last ten feet between himself and Naomi, he feels a purpose he has never felt before. His mind clears, and he sees why he is in this very spot today. He understands he must do the Father's bidding, and he doesn't really know what that involves.

Jesus continues toward the pile of rags and kneels upon reaching them. Ever so carefully, Jesus removes the cloth covering Naomi's face, and with compassion and wisdom of the ages, he places his cheek against hers.

Overcome with emotion as he feels for the first time the chill of death against his human flesh, Jesus exhales, breathing out. His warm breath reaches out and touches Naomi's cold skin. He whispers into her ear. words he didn't know existed, words placed in his soul by eternity's wisdom, words meant only for the dead.

"Naomi, your earthly time is not yet come. You are still needed here." Immediately, the warmth and color returns to Naomi's face. Over his shoulder, Jesus can still hear the soft sobs of Daani and sense the lump in Cris's throat.

As he stands, Jesus looks at his friends and says, "Daani, come and see your mother. She is alive!"

Daani cannot believe what Jesus has just said, and wiping the tears and grime from his cheeks, he lunges forward to see his mother's eyes wide open! He falls upon her as love shows its purpose.

Naomi now weeps. Daani barely breathes. Cris is staring in wonder and disbelief over what he has witnessed. Jesus stumbles backward and falls to his knees, overcome by the glory and power that has coursed through his being. He whispers so no one can hear, "Thank You, Father. Your will today is complete."

Jesus knew this event would have an impact on all their lives and relationships. He also knew that his friends had no idea what really happened and what he had done. He knew the heavenly forces in play this day had a definite purpose, but he didn't know what it was yet.

Jesus was content to let the miracle go unnoticed by human eyes at this time. He also knew that he would be speaking with Naomi alone.

Naomi's Sight

After Naomi's miraculous awakening, she takes a greater interest in the boys' activities. Jesus senses she has been given some inexplicable insight of the heavenly realm unseen by humans and always looks at her in wonder.

Naomi didn't remember much of that night and morning other than her dreams now contain some extraordinary images and visions of the boy Jesus. She cannot explain her feelings toward him now. The confusion comes as she simply sees a lad that obviously enjoys the company of her son, yet every time their eyes meet she senses an inexplicable divine connection.

Jesus can sense the questions Naomi has and knows it needs to be addressed. One day, while Cris and Daani were busy just out of hearing, Jesus finds himself looking into the eyes of the woman whose life had been returned by the touch of his breath.

She reaches out to Jesus as only a mother can and pulls him close to her side. He settles comfortably in next to her warm form and waits for the questions to begin. His heart of hearts tells him this is a special time.

Naomi breaks the silence and says, "Tell me, son, why do I see you in my dreams?" Not waiting for an answer, she continues, "Why are you always surrounded by a great light and gleaming swords of fire?"

Jesus is startled at first at the insight she has been given and knows this must have come from above.

He seeks wisdom before answering as he knows his Father is listening with delight. "I have not yet been given the understanding of many things in my life. They have not been shown to me. I too have wondrous dreams that cannot be explained by earthly means."

"Well, Jesus," Naomi continues on, "I think that you are very special, and I cannot tell for sure, but somehow, you are protected by the heavens. I also seem to remember hearing your voice just before I came out of my great sleep and sense somehow you are responsible."

Jesus knows that this revelation cannot yet be made known and simply diffuses the statement by asking his own question. "How could that be possible, Naomi? You know that I am the son of Mary and Joseph. I was born the same night you delivered Daani!"

Naomi hugs Jesus and begins to release her hold on him, saying, "Of course, you are right. Some things are better left unknown for the moment."

Jesus gets up to walk away, and Naomi playfully tugs at his shirt, calling after him. "I'm going to keep my eye on you, Jesus."

Little did Jesus know this is the just the beginning of his life under watchful eyes.

Life on the Run

The trio rarely interacted with each other's families, and they wanted it that way. Oh, they knew the details all right, but it wasn't about home as much as it was about being away from home. This was the theme they came to embrace each time they met. Their lives on the run going by in a blur, wrapped up in one high adventure after another.

One such day, they planned an excursion to the edge of the village, just where the wild begins. They felt safe, as long as they were in sight of dwellings. They were certain a cry for help would be heard if emitted.

Would this be the day they would put that theory to the test? Jesus and Daani walk lazily between rocks and trees, each poking at things with sticks they carried. Cris is above them, jumping from rock to rock and climbing trees as the urge takes him.

As he reaches the tip-top of a spindly tree, Cris exclaims in a heightened tone, "I can see an opening ahead in the rocks! Looks like a cave! Lets' go in and see what's there!"

Jesus and Daani look where he is pointing and respond with, "We'll beat you!" and take off on a dead run. Of course, Cris takes that as a challenge and jumps down, swinging from branch to branch, skinning his arms and legs. As he reaches the ground, his feet are already churning at the thought of a race.

Cris has one advantage; he knows exactly where he has pointed from his high vantage point. He heads directly to the spot while Jesus and Daani run and search and run and search. Cris arrives ahead of his friends, and he certainly would have it no other way.

While he waits trying to catch his breath, Cris can't help but peer into the opening in the rocks. It takes a few seconds for his eyes to adjust and just about the time he can see Daani and then Jesus come skidding up to him in a great cloud of dust.

"Whoa there, fellas!" As Cris pushes back with his butt, he said, "I was here first, and I will be the first to go in."

Daani knows that a cave or any other rocky opening can hold some nasty little creatures and the possibility of a snake or two. He cautions Cris with, "Make sure you can see, and watch out for the creepy crawlies when you put your hands down."

"Yeah," Jesus pipes in, "we'll wait out here."

Jesus has figured there probably wasn't a whole lot of room in there for all of them at once. Besides, if Cris saw something weird or frightening, he'd be backing out of there in a hurry, and Jesus just knew they'd get run over in the process.

As Cris's backside and feet disappear into the crevice, they can see the cloud of dust coming from within and back up just a wee bit. The two on the outside have their imaginations running wild. They figure Cris is heading into the great unknown with no escape. The moments turn into minutes, and the minutes turn into what seems like an eternity for the anxious boys on the outside, looking in.

"Okay", Jesus finally offers, "he's been in there way too long now."

And they couldn't hear anything coming from the opening now. It was way too quiet, way too dark, and way too still in there. Daani and Jesus inch forward toward the opening with their eyes wide open and ears straining, not really knowing what to expect or think.

And what happens next is still up for interpretation. Intent on the opening before them, they are completely caught off guard as the cavity suddenly fills with big white teeth, piercing yellow eyes, and tawny fur!

A lion! As if the materialization of the lion isn't enough, the big cat's roar causes the strength to instantly vaporize and leave their legs. The boys stumble backward in slow motion. The big cat breaks the sunlight with one graceful stride. Daani can sense the great hunter gathering itself for the leap that will put it instantly upon them!

In the blink of an eye, a blur, a shape, appears dropping from above! It lands squarely on the shoulders of the great cat, rolling it, knocking the beast onto its side.

Jesus and Daani scream and so does Cris as he jumps up from the ground no more than three feet from the now upright lion. Cris's moment of triumph and heroism quickly vanishes. The lion stands its ground, growls, and eyes the daring boy.

As all the players in this cat-and-mouse game eye each other, it becomes evident there is somewhat of a stalemate. The boys are frozen in terror at the nearness and ferocity of the big cat. The beast's only concern is getting away.

Both sides instinctively know that any act of aggression will have dire consequences at this point. An eternity seems to pass when suddenly, the cat relaxes just a little and begins backing away ever so slowly.

The boys don't dare breathe let alone speak, and they are certain they can't run. All their strength is consumed by simply standing as still as possible at this point. Then they watch their adversary of the moment lengthen the distance between them, and soon, silently, disappear into the rocky surroundings. They collapse!

Unsure whether to laugh or cry or both, they stare at each other and then begin slapping Cris on the back and laughing. Jesus and Daani both burst out with, "I cannot believe you did that!"

"Did you really jump on the back of that lion?"

"How'd you get up there?"

"Where'd you go?"

"We were lookin' for you!"

"Are you hurt?"

"You're bleeding!"

"Man! You gotta be kidding me!"

The revelry continues until they are exhausted and realize they better move from their proximity to the rocky opening.

So they run. And run. And run. They end up at the hide. Both Jesus and Daani bow at the waist in grand fashion as they near the hide's opening and wave Cris in with long sweeping motions of their arms.

"After you, O great lion tamer!" Daani jokingly blurts out.

Jesus pokes him in the ribs with his elbow and then says, "You know you really did save us today Cris. Thank you."

As they all assume their positions on the ground in the hide, Cris is finally able to tell the duo what really had happened. As he crawled out of sight into the rocks, it had gotten pretty dark, so much so that he considered turning around and coming back out. Just about the time he was going to turn around, Cris saw a glow, a shaft of light not too far ahead, and decided to continue.

As he reached the light, the crawl space opened up a bit into a larger room—a cave. As soon as he entered the cave, Cris sensed something wasn't right. When he glanced around, he noticed strewn about all sorts of bones and horns of animals he was familiar with. Another thing he noticed was the smell.

Rotting flesh, both fresh and old kills, of an obviously large meat-eating animal lay everywhere, and he was in the middle of its den! Uncertain what to do, his mind was quickly made up as he could hear something coming from way down the passage across the other side of the cave. He knew he could not beat whatever was coming into the cave by returning the way he had come, and he lifted his head to the source of light from above. It was steep, but he figured he could climb up and out quicker than he could crawl back.

Up he went, hoping all the while he was climbing that the opening at the top was large enough to let him through. The way Cris figured it, the lion came into the lair and could smell his scent in the other passage and went to investigate.

The lion followed its nose to the other opening that at that very moment was occupied by Daani and Jesus looking in. Cris had reached the top of the light shaft and knew he had to get to his friends and tell them the fantastic details of his crawling experience fast. As he approached where he thought they would be, he slowed down on purpose.

He figured he'd scare his buddies. If he could just sneak up on them without them seeing him. As he snuck to the edge of the rock above the passage opening and peered over sure enough, there they were. Jesus and Daani were edging closer to the opening.

31

Suddenly, he noticed them stiffen and could hear their united gasp as they clumsily backed away from something he could not see. He was just about to jump up and yell something unintelligible when he heard the roar and saw the lion glide into the picture.

After studying the tense situation for all of a split second, he flew into action, literally flinging himself over the rock, in an arc, ending in the jaws of certain death. Cris thought he was in the air for an eternity and feared his jump might miss the mark when suddenly, the shoulders of the beast appeared perfectly beneath his feet, and they connected with a crunch. The force of the landing on an unstable, uneven lion caused him to pitch sideways and roll as he hit the ground. In the process, he pushed the lion in the opposite direction, creating one really amazing and deadly standoff.

"Man, that is a crazy story!" Daani says. "I wouldn't believe it for a second if I hadn't been there."

Jesus offers some sanity to the moment when he says, "We have all been protected for a reason. Perhaps God has something grand for us all to complete someday."

"Yeah, right, Jesus, maybe you, but not us," quipped Cris as he fingers the scrapes on his arms and legs.

There would be no way he would tell the others how he had really gotten them. For now, they were the evidence that he had fought a lion and survived!

Oh, how they wished that very moment would stick with them forever. As they looked around the dusty circle of life, the smile and gusto was evident as they pushed and shoved each other with glee. They had gone through another life-altering adventure together and survived. Better for the experience and no worse for the wear, they reveled in the moment—united, devoted, inseparable, brothers for eternity.

Age of Responsibility

As these adventures accumulated in their lives, the inevitable reality that they were getting older was also obvious. Life soon began to get in the way of their childhood wanderings and play, and responsibility was taking its place. As ten and then eleven years of age came, it was harder and harder for them to break away from the chores of the family and errands and tasks accompanying everyday life.

And then there were the physical changes beginning to take place. Each boy no longer wore the vestige of childhood. They were young lads now, beginning to take shape as young men. Little did they know that the time of their lives growing up had also prepared them for the next path stretching ahead. They would soon find out that decisions before, that dealt with "whether to jump from the tree or how far to go today," have suddenly turned in to, "don't leave your brother alone for a second," and "I'm counting on you to..." So long, lackadaisical days of childhood!

As Jesus got older, Mary counted on him more to help his dad with projects around the house. And Joseph looked to his son to begin coming with him on small jobs to better understand his trade. It was a task that Jesus took to in earnest, yet his heart longed for the freedom he experienced with his close friends.

Down the street a-ways, Cris was feeling the pressure from his mom to be more of a help around the house, which of course meant more responsibility with his brothers and sisters. It is not that he didn't like the smaller members of the family; it's just that they were so demanding, and he truly missed the freedom of the threesome.

This family stuff really cut into his life on the run, and it didn't sit well with him one bit.

Across town and wherever they could find shelter, Naomi and Daani didn't really have anything to worry about. That is only if you call not having a permanent residence or money enough to buy food or clothing on a regular basis "anything." Naomi sometimes felt as if it would be easier for them to just give up and fade away from life all together, but Daani would have none of that. He loved life, and he loved his mother more. He always reminded her that he could not go on without her. No matter how bad it got for them on the streets, they still had each other. Besides, hadn't God always made sure they had enough to survive?

Moving on and Up

It was a grave day they met at the hide. A day they figured might come yet unspeakable in their minds and thoughts. Their lives would never be the same again. The life that they had always known was about to change.

Jesus has called them together to tell his friends that his family was leaving Bethlehem for good. They are to move as soon as possible back to their hometown of Nazareth. This news strikes to the very quick of their hearts. While it is not fashionable for teenage boys to show their emotions so openly, this hurt deeply, and it was evident.

Jesus is undeniably the hub in their wheel of life. Jesus has always proven to be the guide to keep them straight and served as their group conscience. How could this be happening? Had they not committed themselves to each other and the brotherhood? What would Cris and Daani do on their own? What would Jesus do without them?

Nobody knows me better than my friends.

Jesus offers some consolation that frankly fell on deaf ears, "My dad's work and family in Nazareth are really putting the pressure on us to move back there. Besides, Nazareth is not all that far away, and there will be plenty of times when we see each other."

At that comment, both Daani and Cris look up from drawing scribbles in the sand with their fingers and say, "Yeah right."

Daani feels as if he is losing his mom all over again, and Cris is so upset he becomes angry. "You can't do this to us!" he laments. "We'll never see each other again, and it's just not fair!" Daani cannot bear to think about it any longer and stands from the circle and walks away. He doesn't want his tears to be so apparent. Jesus can see the shoulders of his friend heave up and down, and his own throat begins to tighten with grief.

Unable to speak, Jesus hangs his head in sorrow too. It is Cris now who softens as he scoots over next to Jesus and pushes against his shoulder. "Aw come on, J, I'm not mad at you! It's just that you sprang this on us all at once, and we don't like it one bit, ya know?"

Yes, Jesus knew.

He senses that this meeting has profound ramifications for all of their lives. He senses his deeper, divine calling using this experience as a picture of things and events to come. His Father has placed an ache in his heart recently. A different kind of longing is now replacing his boyhood yearning for gambol and frolic. The Father's longing was that Jesus would be about His business and soon.

A heavenly timetable has suddenly given earthly purpose to Jesus's life. What that ordained was not quite clear to him yet. Although he is pretty sure it will have everlasting importance in shaping the world, Jesus is not ready to comprehend it. His depth of understanding is not complete. Jesus suspects that this too is one of the reasons that they would be returning to Nazareth for sure.

Finality of the Moment

The inevitable day comes, and all the earthly possessions of the small Jewish family are lashed to the backs of a couple of donkeys that pull loaded two-wheeled carts. The four-or-five-day passage to Nazareth is about 80 miles in length and beset with trials and uncertainties. This journey will be much different than the one that brought Mary and Joseph to Bethlehem. Mary will not be riding a donkey this time as she had done on her entry to Bethlehem. The mother of the Savior to-be will be walking and carrying a load of a different nature, unseen.

As the small caravan readies for the trip, the weather seems promising enough for them to be considering the departure. And as the adults gather in the street in front of their home of the past years, the trio gathers just around the corner, out of sight.

This meeting is to be their last in Bethlehem and, as far as at least two of them thought, the last meeting forever. It is a melancholy setting with no one wishing to say the words *good-bye, so long, fare-well, see you later.* Each knew the words would carry a weight they are not ready to shoulder. Not just yet.

They all silently pray for wisdom and words that would belie their preteen years, but nothing seems to come. They stand fidgeting, kicking dust piles with their feet. No one wants to make eye contact as they just know it would lead to words, and words would lead to emotion, and emotion to the end.

Jesus finally looks up. His posture signals it is the time for the beginning of the end. He stops moving. His shoulders slump forward. Jesus realizes he must be the one to break the silence.

"You guys have always been there for me. We've done so much together and learned so much from each other. You are my best friends. We are as close as brothers could ever be." Jesus stops and looks at Cris and then Daani in the eyes. Not caring that they will see the sadness in his own face, he continues, "This parting will only serve to make it more special the next time we meet."

Speaking next, Daani says, "I know that I will never forget you, Jesus, and I'm sure we'll hear more about you and what you are doing. You will always have a special place in my heart and the memories of growing up together will be always on my mind. We have an unbreakable bond."

As the last member of the triad begins to speak, there was a noticeable chink in the indomitable armor of Cris's persona. He gathers himself, and nothing came out when first he opened his mouth. Running the back of his arm across his mouth, he tries again and, this time, manages to say, "You know, J, everything that Daani just said goes for me too. And besides, I'm sure you have something special to do with your life. Maybe all that stuff you been telling us about your dreams and visions is true, and you will be guided by and protected by someone or something much bigger than us."

Wow, Jesus thought, *Cris had been paying attention during those many times we would talk when we were just being lazy and not chasing lions and such.*

Jesus smiled to think of the very real connection the three of them have made in their young lives. This fulfilling thought is rudely interrupted by the call from around the corner. It was Mary. "Jesus, Jesus, it is time to be going. Jesus, do you hear me? We have to leave now!"

The smack of life lands squarely on their faces, and the recoil seems noticeable to each of them. As they shuffle around the corner, they notice all eyes are focused in their direction. It feels as if they are marching stride for stride to their own execution, and the spectators are gathered in hushed silence to see their reaction. All the well-wishers and family friends are collected to send the troupe off on their life- changing journey.

There certainly must have been chatter and talk as the boys approached the gathering, but none of them could hear a word that was spoken. Jesus takes his place among his family as the group begins to move ever so slowly, first in jerks and jostles then in unison as the donkeys find their rhythm.

Cris and Daani stand looking after the entourage as they move away. Jesus breaks from the neat line of travel and stands to the side looking back. The comrades' eyes meet for one long last gaze. Jesus touches his hand to his heart and waves. He turns around and slowly steps back into the tracks being left by the travelers.

He does not turn his back on his friends as much as he turns to face his destiny. His heart breaks as he realizes that in leaving, he forces his friends to their destiny also. He wonders if they have any idea what lay ahead for them.

Beginning Again

Cris and Daani know this will be a true test of their alliance, and they are determined to not let the loss of Jesus from their midst undermine all they have as friends. They are both sure it will hurt deeply the first couple of times they met without Jesus, but go on, they must. They need each other now more than ever before. The streetwise kid with brazen reddish hair and the tough dark-headed kid seemingly with a chip on his shoulder—what buddies.

Cris and Daani both know their parts in this relationship and kept wisely to them. Daani, smart and wise about the way things happen in a small town, and Cris, not afraid to poke his nose into dark corners. Indeed, they needed each other.

The days they are able to get away and spend time exploring and traipsing to stay in focus and are enjoyable. The days they are expected to be in town and around their families now was a different story, however. Cris especially was troublesome at home. He is at that stage in life that no matter what he does, he seems to be in the way. Right, wrong, or indifferent, it doesn't seem to matter.

His parents grow increasingly agitated with his actions and lack of involvement with his siblings and home life. This all suited Cris just fine as he didn't need much of a reason to take off, out the door. Even without Daani tagging along, Cris finds strength in the freedom of being on his own and doing his own thing. Cris's perchance has always been to be a loner, but it seemed that when Jesus was around, he was always kept in the mix and out of trouble.

It is a lot easier for him to entertain his wilder side now, and Daani can see that this was heading in a direction he was not happy with. As they walk away from Cris's house one day, Daani can sense that it must have been one of those testy times at home.

"Had a tough time this morning, Cris?" Daani asks.

"Yeah," Cris answers. "I'd rather not talk about it, though. I really got mad at my mom, and I'm gonna be in big trouble when Dad gets home. That is if I even go home tonight."

"Are you kidding me, Cris?" Daani can't help from saying. "You can always stay with us, wherever that will be."

"I guess we'll consider that when we get to that point later. Let's just get outta here for now." They trudge off in the direction of the center of town with no course of action set in their mind. They both thought as they start out, *Let's see what today brings, and we'll take it from there!*

New Beginnings: Nazareth

The road to Nazareth is long and dusty and keeps stretching on forever so it seems. To complicate matters even more, the family has to spend four nights on the road. This in itself is a major undertaking, and Joseph fears for his family every time they leave the beaten path to set up camp.

God, however, smiles favorably upon their travels and provides protection around about them. Jesus finds it really peaceful and fulfilling to be out at night under the stars. He enjoys the evening hours as they set up camp and ready for the night's stay. The rest of the family seems on edge and are very happy when everything is prepared for the night's stopover and happier when the new morning arrives. Every night, Joseph will tell everyone to be extra vigilant as they rest.

But Jesus knows everything will be just fine. And so their travels end one midday at the village of Nazareth in Galilee. There was no fanfare or welcoming party or any noticeable recognition by anyone as the small band plodded to their new home. The dwelling place had been arranged weeks in advance and is perfect for the new occupants.

In a day or two, everything is unloaded and inside where it belongs, and life returns to normal for the time being.

Dilemma

As the duo walk aimlessly toward the center of town, the thought of visiting the hide hadn't even entered their minds. Their special place somehow didn't seem quite as special with Jesus gone from their midst. Perhaps, that would change soon, but for now, it stood for what they used to have, and the memories were just too fresh.

Absorbed in the nothingness of the moment, they both are caught off guard as the lazy afternoon's silence is broken by a high-pitched scream. It trails off into a sorrowful wail. Frozen in their tracks for a split second, the blood drains from their faces, and their hearts instantly race, imploring them to leave! They soon realize the blare has come from between the buildings they are now motionless in front of.

Their instincts tell them to move! There is, however, something in the instant that begs them to stay.

Finally, Daani grabs Cris's arm while at the same time shouting, "Let's go!" As they enter the alley, they skid to a stop as they realize they cannot clearly see in the dimness the alley provides. Pausing for a second to let their eyes catch up with their feet, the boys see a form in the corner, way back, cowering, as if hiding from something or someone. They approach the form, not knowing what to expect. It moved suddenly as if to shield itself from impending harm and wailed again!

At that moment, the boys should have run like the wind, but they are frozen in place like statues. As the bundle of clothes revealed its occupant, they are startled to find a young girl staring at them from the mass. She has a terrified look on her face, and they can see blood running from the corner of her eye and nose.

Daani gasps at the pathetic sight in front of them, and Cris holds out his hand as if to say *It's okay, we won't hurt you.* Cris stammers slightly, "Are...are you okay? What's the matter? What's wrong?"

She sobs as they inch closer and closer. In a broken, wavering voice, the girl whispers, "Is he still here? Did you see him?"

Daani quickly glances over his shoulder back toward the entrance and says, "Who? Where?"

The girl whispers, "The man, the one that beat me."

As the boys slowly begin to fully take in the situation surrounding them, they notice they are not in a dead-end alley as they had thought. The corner where the girl lays bunched up has another alleyway to the right, leading around the back of the next building.

This would explain why the boys had not seen anyone in the alley from the street out front. As this new bit of information makes its way to their muscles and minds, Cris instantly realizes the danger they are in and no longer is completely concentrating on the injured girl. He starts to take in the entirety of their surroundings and plots the quickest way out of the alley.

The girl is unmoving and seems unwilling to abandon the corner where she at least has her back protected. The boys feel they cannot leave her in this situation and begin pleading with her to get up and move.

"Come on, let's go!"

"We really should get out to the street!"

"Please get up!"

As they plead with the girl, they also know the longer they stay in the darkened alley, the more dangerous the situation becomes for all of them. Soon, their fears are realized as the alley to the right fills with a hulking shadow that blocks the light even more. Both boys whirl to face the unknown.

In turning from the girl, they block the alley shoulder to shoulder in width. The man grows larger with each step he takes forward and quickly fills the alley with his presence a mere ten feet from the boys. A voice they have only heard in nightmares bellows out, "What are you two doing here? Get out of my way! Now!"

Knowing full well the horrific intent of this stranger, they stand their ground, not flinching a muscle. Too frightened to speak, they sense the resolve of each other, ready to face the danger before them to protect the frailty behind them. What that means at the moment, they have no idea, but their very core tells them to stand.

And stand they did! They both are surprised at the swiftness of the adversary as he lunges at them with arms spread wide. A growl seems to come from the center of the man's being as he closes the distance instantly! The boys notice the pungent scent of bad wine just before the impact is felt.

Knocked from their feet in unison, Daani ends up nearly on top of the huddled girl and is able to breathe out, "Run!" as he struggles to regain a breath and footing.

Cris has not fared much better in the intense rush but quickly regains his footing between the girl, Daani, and the man. The look on the man's face is one of satisfaction and gloating as he stands unscathed before the trio. He raises his arm to strike Cris with a downward blow, and Cris darts between his legs and makes it! Scrambling to his feet behind the giant, he has no idea what will happen next.

Daani makes his mind up for him as he screams and rushes the opponent head down and arms flailing. He is met with the mighty blow that had been meant for Cris hitting him between the shoulder blades, instantly knocking him down and out. Daani lays motionless. Cris sees a slight opportunity to attack, and that is what he does, landing on the broad back of the beast. Unable to find any place he can hold on to, he grabs a handful of hair and pulls himself higher toward the head. As the invader tries in vain to grab Cris and rid himself of this last combatant, he stumbles and falls forward onto his knees. This puts Cris in a position to get both his arms all the way around the thick neck.

Able to clasp his hands, Cris pulls with all his might. He pulls and pulls and pulls. He is about to pass out from holding his breath when he feels the mass beneath him suddenly go limp. Drained of all strength and numb from the exertion of the struggle, Cris strains to stand and make sense of what lays before him. Gathering his wits for a moment, he frantically searches for Daani and the girl.

He sees a foot sticking out from underneath the fallen man and frantically tugs and pushes to get the huge body off Daani. In the midst of jostling, the man begins to moan and awaken! Cris is terrified to think the enemy will wake up and desperately looks for an advantage. There it is, lying a few feet from the struggle—a broken chair leg!

Lunging for the club, he springs to his feet just as the adversary struggles to his hands and knees. Acting on survival instinct, Cris jumps and swings the club in one motion. The club connects solidly with the side of the man's head with a crack that startles Cris with its sharpness.

The man drops without a sound. The silence of the instant is astonishing as Cris slumps to the ground himself motionless. Soon, he hears his own heart beating loudly. Then he hears Daani's unnerving gasps for air and then hears his moan. This jostles Cris to his feet and restores the purpose of the moment. Cris rushes to Daani's side and pulls him to his feet.

As Daani regains his breath and vision, he blurts, "Where's the girl? Did she get out? Did you see her?"

Cris cannot answer any of these questions and shrugs his shoulders in response. It is then Daani notices the mass of a man blocking the exit to the right alley. Prostrate, motionless, and huge. Cris finally will entertain only one action. "Run! Now!"

They race out the way they had entered the alley. Throwing all abandon to the wind, they hit the sunlight, and they ran. In their rush out of the alley, the boys fail to notice the other travelers they streak past.

Most of them, however, cannot help but observe the boys as they run away.

Knowing

Jesus has been experiencing intense dreams and vivid celestial news since arriving in Nazareth. His understanding of the cosmos and mankind and his purpose is growing in great strides with no end in sight to the knowledge the Father is imparting to his heart.

It is early one morning just after sunrise and his awakening that he kneels beside his bed mat to contemplate his night-time revelations. He is compelled to speak. In a still voice, he breathes out barely audible, "Father, you have blessed me so to entrust in me things that I cannot fully understand until my time has come. I see Your plan beginning to form in my spirit and mind. Give me wisdom and understanding and Your nature as these things are revealed. Father, it is only by Your hand that the world was made and the stars set in place and now this same hand has found pleasure in provision for Your people and their future. Grant me Your vision and Your purpose, and instill in me Your love for all mankind. I trust You now and will trust You when the day comes for the way of deliverance to be made known. Give me strength in knowing You will always be by my side."

As Jesus is in the midst of his solitude with the Father, he becomes aware of another presence. He slowly turns to see the familiar shape of his mother silhouetted in the archway. He smiles knowing the blessing of having his earthly mother as a God-given ally in this heavenly scheme.

Mary senses that what she has just heard a portion of is special and not meant for everyone's ears. She calls to Jesus saying, "Son, Joseph is waiting for you. You know you are supposed to go with him today to finish up that job at the corner house. Don't keep your father waiting."

"So be it," he whispers. He rises to acknowledge his earthly duties as the son of a stone mason. As he passes Mary in the doorway, she purposely stands so that Jesus must brush against her as he walks by. Mary lovingly reaches out and touches her son, her gift from the Most High, stroking his hair. This causes Jesus to pause, and he turns to face his mother. Reaching up to place his hand upon hers and gaze into her face, he smiles.

In an instant, Jesus sees the depth of understanding in her eyes and is for a second in awe at all she really did comprehend. He can see it in her face. He can feel it in her touch. He understands the love and sorrow entwined in her soul and the sacrifice she is to endure when his destiny is revealed. He sees an earthly love unfettered by heavenly will, and he sees it all in the form of a woman willing to accept the Father's direction. As he squeezes Mary's hand, Jesus thinks, "I still have plenty to learn at her feet."

Mary's Wisdom

Her first insight had come to her as a child. Of course, Mary had no idea what it all meant. After all, she is just a youngster of Jewish heritage being raised in the doctrine of her forefathers. Her parents, like all the others, look to the promise of the scriptures and pray for direction for their daughter. The reality of her destiny comes upon her like a thief in the night as she struggles with female adolescence and the place of a woman in the patriarchal society.

Arranged at a very young age to be married to a man much her senior, she is barely ready to leave her given family, let alone be responsible for her own family. Her confidence is bolstered one day as she meets with God's messenger. Her life will never again be the same.

Mary hums softly some unknown tune as she busies herself around the house. It is a clear, sunlit Morning, and the birds chirped and the sounds of life emanate from the light beams themselves. The rest of the family has found other things to attend to outside, out of sight. As she bends to retrieve an errant stone from the dirt floor, she thinks she notices the room brighten. When she straightens, she is startled to see a man in a brilliant white robe standing next to the entrance.

His countenance is unlike any man she had ever seen and is known to exist on earth. He is not threatening or intimidating in any way, and instantly, she feels peace flow over her very being. He speaks so softly she can't hear with earthly ears and hears him through her heart, her spirit.

"Mary." At the sound of her name, she falls prostrate to the floor. "Do not be afraid. I am here that you may understand more fully the station the Father will grant to you in life. The Most High has chosen you to be blessed among all the inhabitants of this world. You will be used to further God's plan for the whole of mankind."

Mary dares not rise or even look at the figure but only whispers, "How can this be as I am but a child myself of common descent, of no accord that none would notice?"

The angel reassures her with a broad sweep of his hand and says, "Your strength and stature and wisdom will increase as you approach the age of awareness. The Father has granted you a loving heart with virtue as your guide. Know this, Mary, I will be with you in all that you say and do. I will never leave your side."

The angel prepares to leave by rising from the floor, floating, suspended. "Do not speak of this to anyone as the time is not fulfilled for the world to know."

As Mary looks on in wonder, the angel ascends through the ceiling and is gone. Mary slowly gathers herself and looks around to see if anyone else has witnessed this event. She is alone. Mary feels her heart leap within her as she struggles to take in all that has just happened. Mary would think many times of this first meeting with the heavenly realm and looked forward to the next instance with great anticipation.

She did not have any idea what possible use YHWH could have with her but was filled with hope.

Teaching and Learning

It comes as no surprise to Jesus that he loves hearing the scriptures read aloud. At home, he always cherishes the evenings the family gathers to read and recite. Mary and Joseph look at these times as a serious educational experience also.

Jesus presents himself as an exceptional student eager and willing to read and study every chance he gets. He notices an attraction, a tugging at his heart every time he strides past the temple in town. Occasionally, he stops to hear the great teachers as they read and discuss the scriptures. One day, when he feels compelled, he raised his hand to be recognized and is given the opportunity to speak.

The teachers sat in rapt attention as this boy addressed the small gathering with wit, wisdom, and insight way too deep to be coming from the teenager. From that day forward, Jesus is a welcome guest anytime he came to attend the discussion, that is, until his heavenly birthright begins to be revealed.

That revelation will one day change everything. Jesus somehow understands that these same teachers will one day condemn him and cast him aside like waste. These same men who now embrace him and his novelty will curse and spit upon him and scream for his death.

Jesus shudders as a coldness runs through his very core, the very same chill he felt when he touched Naomi's cheek with his, and then he understands.

Trouble Begins

The knock on the portico of Cris's house sounds like many others before. This time, however, it comes at the hand of a village official. And he is there on official business.

Ellise finds her way to the front of the house and invites the man in. The man begins describing an incident in town the other day in which another man was attacked in an alley and hurt very badly. It seems the man was beaten and hit in the head with a club and then left for dead. The beaten man described two boys as his attackers. And two teenage boys were seen running from the alley toward this side of the village just about the time of the assault.

Was there a chance he could talk to her son and see if he knew anything about this attack?

Ellise sits there, listening to the narrative of the incident and the description of the boys seen running from the scene, and her heart sinks. She can imagine that Cris lays just the other side of the wall, listening to this whole account, barely breathing. Her mother's intuition tells her that Cris is involved, but her mother's shield will not let her speak it aloud.

Ellise stands from the conversation and says, "Unfortunately, my son is not home at this time, but I'll be sure to speak with him about this when he gets home."

As the town elder heads for the door, he concludes, "Ellise, I'm sure you understand the severity of this incident, and it is very important we get to speak with Cris. I'm sure he had nothing to do with this, but we have to get to the bottom of these very serious allegations and must find who is responsible."

"Yes, yes, I totally agree. Have a nice day."

Her smile for the official quickly vanished as she turns from the porch and heads back inside. Oh, how she dreads finding the truth of this incident and quickly decides to wait for her husband to get home before confronting Cris.

From the other room, Cris hears the whole thing and cannot believe what was said! What about the little girl that was beaten up? They saved her! His blood began to boil as he listened in. Cris stole from the room and silently slipped out a tiny window to the ground below. Once outside, he crept from the area and then burst into a full run in search of Daani.

Cris felt exhilaration as he ran and searched. He couldn't tell whether it was because he was scared to death and high on adrenalin or because he was afraid he wouldn't be able to warn Daani. Cris was sure they would be looking for Daani too at this very moment.

It looked like a lost cause as Cris quickly ran out of places to search. It was then it came to him—the hide! Off he goes on a trot and soon enters the familiar lair. Sure enough, once inside, he finds Daani, but he isn't alone! Cris quickly glances around the interior to see if there are any more surprises, and satisfied, he goes over to Daani.

As he sits next to him, he says, "Hi, Naomi, didn't expect to see you here." Without pausing, he continues, "Brother, I have been looking all over for you! I was afraid they found you already!"

"Found me? Found me for what? Who is looking for me?" Daani says in surprise.

As Cris relates the story of the official's visit to his house this morning, he can't help but notice Naomi squirming as he speaks. He knows that Daani has told her of the episode just by the way she looks. Cris thinks that this may be a good thing already having an adult up to speed on the "incident." Daani cannot believe that the monster man has accused them of attacking him! "That guy is the bad guy, not us!" he laments.

Cris says what they all were thinking, though, "Nobody is gonna believe us over that man."

"Where did the girl go? She can get us out of this! What was her name? Man, we don't even know her name!"

Naomi, indeed, has heard Daani's version of the clash and knows that based on the story the officials are going on, the boys will be in great trouble if identified. She also knows that their only chance is to get Cris's parents involved and make sure they know the real story. They had little more discussion, and what they did have revolved around when Cris thought his father would be home.

Soon, it was off to Cris's house to face the questions, innuendos, and accusations. Cris's dad, Samuel, walked in to a solemn setting on his return home. As he enters the abode, he notices Ellise sitting next to the homeless woman Naomi and both Cris and Daani off to the side cross-legged on the dirt floor with their heads down.

Without even washing the dust of the day from his hands and feet, Samuel takes a seat across the room to better take in all those gathered together. *This must be serious,* he thinks as he sits down.

Ellise begins with the visit from the village elder and the account as given to her. Cris and Daani give the actual scenario in vivid detail. Samuel listens intently. Upon completion of the narrative, Samuel stands with a great sigh, paces to the left and right, thinking, and then he plops back down in his seat, shoulders slumped forward.

He looks intently at all the participants and summarizes, saying, "So, we have a moody kid with chip on his shoulder and a homeless kid with no real place to live that are known to run around together that were seen running from an attack on a man in an alley. The boys say they were protecting a girl that the man beat up and left bloody and hurt in the alley, and the man says he was just plainly attacked by two boys and left for dead. The girl is nowhere to be found and is unknown. Am I missing anything here? Anyone?"

"No, well, there you have it. We are going to go to the court and tell our side of the story and face the accuser and hear his."

"This will come about as soon as I can make an appointment with the court."

At that, the meeting was over for the time being. Dread filled all the hearts of the adults as they know it looks very bad for the boys. The boys, however, knew the truth. They were there and could not

LEFT CROSS, RIGHT CROSS

believe that they had done anything wrong. The elders would surely see that!

Cris walks Naomi and Daani out on the porch. The night air is beginning to knock the heat from the buildings, and evening stars are showing their early glimmer.

"Are you two going to be all right tonight?" he asks as they step from the light and into the street.

As they disappeared into the growing darkness, he hears Naomi's voice drift across the night air, "We'll manage just fine."

Cris enters the house, uncertain of what to expect from his parents. He walks past the doorway into the eating area, and he pauses to see Samuel facing the doorway with Ellise holding tightly in his arms. She sobs uncontrollably. Samuel motions with his hand for Cris to keep going. Cris hangs his head and continues on to his room, distraught to see his mother in such despair.

Mary's Interlude

Jesus prepares a few food staples, a bedroll, and some water in a goat skin. The watchful eye of Mary notices his preparations, and she soon sides up to her son.

"Planning a trip, Jesus?" Mary asks. Already fully aware that her son must one day break from human routine to pursue his godly purpose, she shudders to think the day might have arrived.

Jesus nods and says, "Mary, you of all people know that I must be about my Father's business and search for all He has for me to embrace. I cannot grow in the Father's wisdom tied down with the bonds of human need. I must learn at the Father's feet, in His presence, face-to-face. Surely you understood that this day would come, and I would be gone for a time."

Taking the face of Jesus in her hands, she places her cheek next to his, relishing the warmth, the embrace, and the nearness. A tear forms and runs down her cheek. Its descent joins the surfaces in oneness. Jesus feels the bonding of this human flesh and is moved beyond strength, slowly sinking to his knees. He rests his head on her thigh. Mary strokes his hair, and Jesus weeps. No words are needed.

Into the Wild

Jesus has learned at an amazing pace. His understanding of the scriptures and the known world seems too full for a young man who has attained the age of sixteen years. The maturity in body matches his ability to reason and speak. His curly brown hair reaches past his shoulders now, and his gray eyes have a steely blue tint. The rounded shoulders of youth are replaced by the hardened shoulders of a laborer, and his soft hands have taken on the coarseness of use. Gone are flat smooth muscles replaced by sinewy chords of strength.

All the ages have pointed to this time of maturity in human flesh. Jesus will need every ounce of strength and wile to return to his destiny. This is fitting for a young man who is about to trek into the wild and leave his family and all he has ever known behind. The direction Jesus has been given is strong in his spirit, and it leads away from the comforts he is accustomed to.

His time for solitude and greater understanding has arrived. He has reached the age of accountability and must now choose to accept the road less traveled. He must embrace the lifestyle of a wanderer and show allegiance to none on earth. To fully welcome the nature of his godhead, his mind must be free from distraction and human impediment. He must learn the limitations of his earthly form to better comprehend the divinity that courses through his veins. If Jesus can embrace everything the Father has given him to bear and his physical being is able to withstand the onslaught, he will be ready for the Father's bidding.

The bedroll is slung over his shoulder, his sandals laced tightly, and food enough for a week is placed neatly in a linen sack. As Jesus steps off the porch, he heads toward the edge of town. Once there, he sees the used, beaten path heading north leading to Tyre and beyond. He turns and heads east into the desert and into the wilderness. Jesus separates from his earthly family in order to find his heavenly lineage.

With each stride, Jesus leaves the footprint of a man. Upon his return, he will leave the prints of a lamb.

Day of Court

Everyone was anxious for the day in court to arrive. Now that the day has finally come, however, they are not so eager to learn exactly what destiny has in place for Cris and Daani.

Both families have gathered together at Samuel and Ellise's to walk as a group to the village center to the court. As they approach the hub of town, there is no small talk as each family has played this scene over in their minds hundreds of times. Daani and Cris are the only ones who have pictured a just end to the day's events. The parents of the boys have figured this will end badly.

The court proceedings are to be held in an open-air setting with the town elders to the north end of a walled courtyard. There are three archway entrances to the courtyard that rise above the short walls one each—in the south, east, and west walls. The men who will hear the proceedings are seated with their backs to the taller solid north wall.

There are no other seats provided within the courtyard. From each flat section in the wall, wooden uprights with angled supports extend out with tapestry stretched between to provide shade for those gathered. If filled to capacity, the venue would hold nearly one hundred people. On this day, the assembly is packed to overflowing, and many onlookers are forced to sit atop the short walls themselves. These proceedings have caused quite a stir in the village as the accusations are severe and have life-changing implications.

The families of Cris and Daani make their way through the throng and approach the front table. They all sit cross-legged in the dirt before the court. Cris and Daani anxiously look about to see if they can spot the man who had terrorized them in the alley. He was not in their sight.

The lead elder, a man named Jonah, clears his throat in an effort to get everyone's attention, and the din of the gathering seems to increase. Jonah stands to his feet and slams a wooden slat down on the tabletop causing quite a loud *thwack!*

Instantly, the multitude becomes silent and focuses on the elder. Jonah does not address the crowd but looks directly at Cris and Daani, saying loudly, "Young men, stand and come near to the table."

The abruptness of the salutation catches them both off guard, but they quickly jump to their feet and take a couple of steps forward. As the young men stand before the table, they appear calm and in control. Cris is dressed in a tightly woven shirt that hangs to his knees light-blue in color with the sleeves gone, exposing his thickly muscled shoulders and arms. Around his waist is a bright-red sash knotted in the middle. His sandals have long leather straps that wrap up and around his calf muscles tied off just below his knees. His dark hair is neatly trimmed and brushed as usual.

Daani stands next to Cris and is in stark contrast to the neat, crisp package that Cris presents. Daani wears a clean but tattered light-brown shirt with noticeable holes here and there. It too hangs to his knees. Around his waist he wears a thick rope tied in a square knot with the frayed ends hanging loosely in front. His shirt too is without sleeves that expose his sinewy tight shoulders and arms. Daani is wearing flat pieces of hide for sandals that are tied with leather around his ankles. Daani's chestnut hair hangs loosely around his shoulders and frames his tanned face perfectly. Daani glances at Cris and smiles as their eyes meet, proud to be standing next to his best friend.

Jonah was still standing, and now has the boys in front of the bench. He looks directly at them and proceeded, "You both have been accused of a serious offense. You will be allowed to tell your side of the story once the hearing begins. Before that happens, your accuser will come forward and bring the accusations against you. Do you understand?" Both boys nod yes. "Sit back down."

Jonah looks to the west entrance and calls out, "Bring in Cain that he may make the charges." All eyes swing to the west as the archway is darkened by the accuser—a mountain of a man named Cain.

As he plods forward to the table, the boys instinctively scooted back. Cain glances down to the boys as he approaches and sneers at them, showing brown teeth and the fresh red scar along the side of his forehead. He centers himself in front of the table and stands shoulders slouched forward, feet planted and sways slightly like an oak tree in a breeze. Cain leans in, placing his hands on the table, instantly causing a noticeable dip in the wooden surface.

Looking squarely into the face of Jonah, he grumbles, "I'm here."

Cain is instructed to begin with his account of the attack that day. The clash in the alley is described in detail just as it happened. Everything except for the reason Cain was in the alley in the first place—to rape and finish off the little girl he had left bloody and beaten.

"I was minding my own business, taking a short cut through the alley, when the boys jumped me and knocked me in the head," with that, Cain concluded. Cain lumbers off to the side, relinquishing the limelight.

Cris and Daani get up and approach the table to stand once again before the court. Confident in their story, Cris begins with, "It's pretty much as he said, except that we heard a scream come from the alley and went in to find this little girl all beat up and bloody. While we were trying to get her out of the alley into the street"—Cris points directly at Cain—"he came back and started the fight! We weren't going to let him get to the girl again."

Jonah was already familiar with both sides of the account, and the proceedings were the public airing of the sequence of events and accusations. Jonah stands to address the boys and the crowd. "At this time, bring out the girl that was in the alley to justify your story."

Cris and Daani look hopelessly at each other, and Daani offers, "We don't know where she is or who she is. She ran away during the fight."

He whirls and points at Cain, yelling, "He is lying about the girl. We were protecting her from him!"

At that the crowd begins murmuring and whispering so much so that Jonah has to slam the wooden slat down again to get everyone's attention. He continues, "This hearing is now concluded with both sides being presented. This court will return a ruling in one hour."

The three elders leave the courtyard to decide the fate of Cris and Daani. Needless to say, this will be the longest hour of the boy's life as they huddle together to await for the decision. The crowd seems to increase as word is relayed about town that the court will gather again in an hour for the outcome.

The elders enter through the east archway, their long robes flowing as they make their way to the table. Once behind the table, they all remain standing to face the boys, their families, and the crowd. Cain stands off to their left, also in front of the crowd.

Jonah motions for the boys to stand, and they do. "Come forward. After hearing both sides of the incident and being that the boys cannot produce a witness to testify to their side of the story, this court rules on the side of Cain. He was attacked by these two and injured and left for dead. Further, the court finds that the boys shall each be given fifteen lashes and held in the village jail for sixty days. This punishment shall be administered immediately."

Naomi has remained silent as has Ellise through the entire proceedings. She now begins sobbing softly and covers her head with her shawl to hide her grief. Ellise reaches out and puts her arm around her shoulder, and they both weep. The boys are led out through the west archway toward the center of town where the village square is located.

The crowd follows. It is here a heavy wooden post is rooted in the ground with leather straps fastened to the top. As the lads approach the square, they knew well enough the purpose of the post and can see bloodstains upon it as they draw near.

Made to stand before the post, their upper torso is laid bare to the waist as their shirts are pulled over their shoulders. Cris and Daani are taken to opposite sides of the post and tied with their hands together above their heads, facing each other. The man with the whip approaches, and the crowd parts to let him through.

Daani whispers to Cris while the man advances, "It'll be okay. Just keep looking at me."

The man begins on Daani's side of the post. The crowd now surrounds the post, ready to witness the gory side of justice meted out. They back away from the punisher when he faces the boys and the whipping post. The man wears a bloodstained leather apron over his robe, and a mask covers the lower portion of his face from his nose to his neck. As the arm holding the whip is raised above his head, the crowd yells out in unison, "One!"

The swipe brings the whip in contact with Daani's bare back. Daani is surprised at the force and the pain this narrow lash and knots inflict. His knees buckle slightly. "Two!" came the shout as the stinging is unbroken. "Three!" Unrelenting. "Four!" Unceasing.

By the shout of nine or ten, Daani has mercifully passed out from the torment of the beating. He is unaware when the man reaches fifteen lashes, and his full body weight is already hanging from his wrists. Cris can hardly bear to watch.

But he does notice the whip. With each strike, it tears into Daani's belly as it wraps around his torso before being withdrawn. *This is going to be bad,* Cris thinks.

The whipping man wastes no time in moving to Cris's side of the post as soon as he finished on Daani. Daani's blood drips from the leather strap as he walks. The whipping man shuffles and drags the whip's tendrils in the dust. Cris squeezes his eyes shut tight when he hears the shout of, "One!"

Whew, that wasn't so bad, Cris thought.

"Two!" With rugged determination, Cris hangs as each stripe is laid upon his back.

The torment lasts for what seems an eternity and then is over at "Fifteen!" Cris has counted them all. He is weakened as never before and struggles with all his might to remain standing. He feels the blood beginning to pool around his waist where it soaks the sash. As he stands amid the misery of the moment, he instinctively reaches around the post to grasp Daani's hand.

It is cold. Cris shakes his hand and feebly calls to his friend, "Daani! Daani! It's over. It's over. It is finished!"

At that, Daani opens one eye to look up at his friend and fights to his feet, pushing off from the post. They stand together once again. The crowd begins to disperse as soon as the whipping concludes. Naomi and Ellise are allowed to go and release the bindings from their wrists and dress the bloody welts with salve. Some of the cuts are torn deep into their once smooth skin.

The boys are wrapped in torn cloth strips to cover the wounds. When the mothers have done all they can to ease the pain and cover the wounds, they gently raise the boys' shirts over their shoulders, wincing as they pass over each welt.

No sooner has their shirts been put back in place the blood from beneath begins soaking through. Naomi cries openly as she notices the blood on the outside of the shirt. Unable to stem the flow, she feels helpless. Ellise also sobs as she sees the blood soaking through. She shudders to think of what truly lays underneath.

"Samuel, Samuel!" she calls, "Bring me your overcoat!"

Samuel stumbles forward, removing his jacket as he came. Ellise grabs it and, with strength, found in agony rents it in two with one motion, handing one half of the garment to Naomi and gently placing the other half around the shoulders of Cris. It is all she can think to do.

This last act of love is doubly important. They will need the extra covering as this will also be their first night in a cold, damp jail cell.

Part of the Land/Solitude

Jesus doesn't turn around as he walks with the setting sun over his shoulder. The fading warmth of the day will soon take on the coolness of the evening and then the chill of night. Jesus smiles as the visible effect of the sun fades. He knows this will be the first night of an important, new beginning in his adult life.

Contented he has travelled far enough for one day, he notices a rocky outcropping just ahead and heads that way. He gathers enough wood and sticks to build a fire, and he detects the last orange streaks of the evening sky fading from view. He wonders if the Father has placed them there just for him to enjoy.

Then he laughs to himself at that thought. Of course, the Father has placed them there for all to notice if they so choose. That thought brings a smile to his face. Jesus is content this first night to unroll his pack, have a piece of hard bread, and a drink of water before lying down. He stretches out on his back and his hands clasped beneath his head. He notices the moon showed a bright sliver of itself, and the stars glimmered. The fire is comforting as it dances before him.

He closes his eyes. The new day creeps over the ridge and catches Jesus snuggled tightly in his bedroll. The fire has died in the night, and his sleep was so sound he didn't even notice.

He has, however, a foreboding in his heart he cannot explain as his thoughts turn to Bethlehem and his first home. Jesus packs his bedroll, and he thinks of his friends, Cris and Daani, and wonders. As Jesus walks away from his first camp, he faces east, and the sun licks his face. The new day is peaceful in its beginning, and Jesus wonders if it will stay that way. He also wonders if this is what this entire time of discovery is supposed to be like—wondering. Wondering and not knowing? Wondering without answers?

As these thoughts cross his mind, he noticeably picks up his walking pace in agitation. He hurries with no destination in mind. Then he notices the lace on his sandal has become unraveled and stoops to attend to it. As he pauses on one knee, he hears, "There!"

He lifts his head to see who is speaking to him. No one or anything is near to where he kneels. Jesus moves to stand, and the voice is heard again, "Stay!"

Not quite understanding what is happening in the moment, Jesus stands to look at his surroundings and hears, "Listen!"

There is more urgency in this last declaration, and Jesus takes notice. He falls to his knees and places his forehead on the ground as the morning sun's light focuses on his form. The very ground shakes and shimmers beneath the presence of the light! He is listening now!

The morning light speaks as the One surrounds his being. "You wonder without taking heed. You seek without opening your eyes. You search before you ask.. What am I to do with you, son?"

"Father!" The assertion comes easy for Jesus, yet it humbles his very soul. He has never in this earthly realm been in the presence of the manifestation of YHWH, and his humanness nearly dissolves.

"Father, I hear You and seek only Your will for my being here." The sunlight laughs at this suggestion. "Then why do you not ask?" And with that, the sunlight has spent its focus and returns its attention to the earth.

Jesus struggles to his feet once again on solid ground—shaken, humbled, wiser. He looks down at his feet and notes the lacing. He smiles. He will never forget the lesson of the untied lace. He places one foot in front of the other and noticed a new devotion in the firmness of his stride.

He wonders what might lay over the horizon. "Father, guide me!"

Bitterness

Cris and Daani cannot tell what hurts more as they are dragged off to the holding cell. The obvious pain from their wounds is present, but the agony in the wails from their mothers cuts to the very core of their hearts. Each shudders as a chill runs through their spine though the heat of the day is quite evident. They both are in a state of disbelief and indignation at the outcome of the day.

How wrong! None of that matters now though as they are pushed and pulled like criminals to their abode for the next sixty days. It is the belly of the beast and stinks like one too. Their destiny unfolds before them, and they find themselves alone in the cell for now. So much the better. They hug the bare damp ground like a long lost friend and try to get comfortable for the first agonizing night in the dungeon. They quickly find there is no comfortable position in their state of injury. The only solace they find is in their closeness as they toss and turn on the floor.

The next morning showed bright but no promise of relief for the pain and discomfort or the betrayal they felt. Perhaps this helped lead to the resolve that they both swore an allegiance to that day. This would never happen to them again.

They would never leave their destiny in the hands of another person or persons. The court of law would never have to deliberate over their fate again. They would determine their own destiny from this day forward. They would leave no doubt about whether an incident was caused by their hand. Their blood was mingled not by their own design or desire.

Cris and Daani aged noticeably this day; they matured. As the blood dried on their backs and the scars formed, hardness replaces trust, and their hearts would soften no more, forevermore.

The rebellious archangel acquires two more soldiers this day, and heaven wept.

Enlightened

Jesus soon finds it necessary to fend for himself as he quickly runs out of food. Now this is something he hasn't really thought out. He has brought his shepherds sling along, and it hangs loosely from his waistband. He has an opportunity to use the sling as he approaches a pile of rocks that seem to rise out of the desert sand from nowhere.

He notices a marmot perched atop the rocks in a perfect silhouette. Retrieving the sling and a few smooth stones, he sneaks as close as he can and waits until the creature seems to look the other way. Slowly rising from his crouch, he twirls the sling about his head and releases the stone! A perfect miss!

The marmot scampers in between some boulders and begins a raspy chastisement of the errant hunter. Jesus smiles because the scolding seems way too loud for such a small creature. "Indeed," he muses. "I must take to heart the importance of practice if I am to eat during this sojourn."

As he walks away, the chatter from the indignant animal grows softer and softer. Now he begins his sling training in earnest. Walking and throwing, walking and throwing. Soon, he has mastered the accuracy he desires and continues on his way.

His travels have taken him far from any village. As he rounds a rocky out cropping one day, he notices a wisp of smoke rising from a distant group of trees. Jesus heads that way to investigate. He approaches as silently as possible. He knows these deserts are known to hold malcontents prone to thievery and mayhem. He stretches his neck above a bush and notices a lone man, an old man with his back to Jesus. This man stoops over, writing in the sand with a stick.

Feeling somewhat safe, Jesus steps out from behind the bush, takes a few steps, and stops.

"Come, Come!" the old man says without turning from his writing. "I've been expecting you, Jesus, son of Joseph and Mary. Come!"

Jesus is caught off guard that this old man would know his name and status out in the middle of the desert! "How, how, do you know my name as I have travelled many miles to arrive at this point, far from any village?" Jesus stammers.

The old man chuckles and slowly rises up to turn and face Jesus. In doing so, he also reveals the startling fact that he is blind! "I know your Father, and He has sent me to watch over and provide for you."

Jesus stumbles. "You know my father Joseph, and he sent you out here to find me?"

The old man chuckles once again and says, "If that will make you feel more comfortable, then yes, that is how I've come to be here." He continues laughing, shaking his head.

Still in wonder, Jesus asks, "How have you travelled all this distance seeing that you are blind and there is no guide?"

"Your Father, YHWH, has seen to it that I have arrived here in your time of searching and wonderment. I simply do His will."

"Sit, sit. You make me weary." With that, the old man plops down on the ground, sitting cross-legged to face Jesus.

Jesus finally hears what the old man is saying and likewise plunks himself down. He finally begins to take in the enormity of this meeting.

The old man begins, "My name is Eli, and I have known this earth before. YHWH has seen fit to have me trod this earth once again, to bring Him glory and so it is."

Jesus's breath is taken from his lips as he realizes this was the high priest Eli who had raised the boy Samuel in the ways of the Lord. This account is written and passed down from generation to generation in Hebrew history, and Jesus knows it well.

Jesus interjects, "Since you know who I am and why I am here, perhaps you can tell me?"

Eli laughs again and says, "Whoa there, son. This knowledge may take some time and getting used to on your part. Besides, YHWH's timetable is perfect, and we must be mindful of His plan for you."

Jesus at once sees his own impatience and says, "Yes, I see, I see."

Eli raises his eyebrows and says, "That is good! That's a start. Now we have a more pressing need at the moment that you should address."

Jesus sits upright at this suggestion, eager to begin learning. Eli continues with, "We need dinner!"

"Let's just see how well you handle that sling in your belt!"

Jesus is beginning to understand that Eli sees a lot more than a person with eyesight and makes a mental note to remember that. Eli waves his hand toward the edge of the trees over his shoulder and says, "Seems to me I heard a guinea in the trees over that way a while back, probably a good place to start."

Jesus jumps up and shakes his head in wonder at this old sage (sure that somehow Eli even saw that) and trots off in that direction, sling in hand. Eli calls after him, "I'll have the fire going good by the time you return."

Wonder of wonders, Jesus thinks, *what else does the Heavenly Father have in store for me?* A smile crosses his face as he slows to a walk and switches into hunter mode, sling at the ready. *A guinea would be great for dinner tonight!* He must see to it that the hunt is successful. *Can't let Eli down.*

Eli stoops over the coals he has just raked from the center of the fire to the outside. His mind's eye sees the form of a perfect cooking spot and nods in satisfaction. Jesus thought he would be funny and try to sneak back into camp without calling to Eli to let him know of his return, but Eli had heard the smooth stone make contact with the guinea and knew of Jesus's eminent return.

Eli calls out to Jesus while he is sneaking his way back. "No sense wasting time there, young man. Get that bird over here! I'm getting hungry!"

With that, Jesus picks up his pace and soon lays the bird next to Eli. The old man eagerly grabs the bird and deftly plucks and dresses it with amazing speed and dexterity. In short order, the bird is on a stick and roasting over the coals. Eli would reach out at seemingly just the right moment to turn the cooking bird to keep it from burning.

Jesus just sits and watches in amazement, and presently, it is ready to eat. As Eli removes the cooked bird from the coals, he looks to Jesus and says, "Let us thank the Father for His provision and for good company!"

With that, Eli lifts his hands toward heaven and offers, "May YHWH give you the desire of your heart and make all your plans succeed. We will shout for joy when you are victorious and will lift up our banners in the name of our God. May the Lord grant all your requests. Amen" (Ps. 20:4–5).

Jesus was fascinated by the prayer and tendered, "You have recited our father David and his plea for Help. May the Father be merciful and hear."

Eli smiles and says, "Oh, He does, He does. It pleases me and the Father that you recalled the scriptures. Perhaps our time together will be productive after all!"

With that, Eli picks up the bird and removes a leg and hands the bird to Jesus, who follows suit. Soon, they are chewing and talking and chewing and talking. As their dinnertime ends, Jesus gets up to gather his bedroll and belongings and passes the spot where he had noticed Eli writing in the sand on his approach—the Hebrew symbols unmistakably form (Yeshua bar Abba), which is to say, "Jesus, son of the Father."

Jesus stops in his tracks and turns to see Eli facing his direction. Eli says, "I told you I've been expecting you."

Downward Spiral

The sixty days in jail prove hard on the friends and hardened more than their muscles. The scabs were gone from their backs now, replaced by hard reddish scars. There are scars much deeper than those evident on their backs, however.

Cris and Daani lost their sense of wonder and childhood that day at the whipping post. The days in jail simply helped solidify the hardness in their hearts. They emerged from the shadows of the dungeon, mere shadows of the trusting young men who had entered.

Ellise and Naomi have both paid regular visits to their sons in jail. They are very aware of the changes this experience has made in them. They could hear it in their voices. They could see it in their posture. They fear the hurt has gone too deep. They fear the damage to their imaginations has thrust them too soon into full adulthood. They fear they have lost their way.

It won't be long until the mother's worse fears are realized. The women meet their sons as they emerge into the light of day from their confinement. The young men walk heads down toward their mothers and into their outstretched arms. The hugs go only one way as the arms of the sons remain at their sides. Naomi reaches up and gently lifts Daani's chin to look in his face and kiss his cheek. He then softens a little and manages a half-smile that quickly vanishes.

Cris will have nothing of an emotional exchange and quickly escapes Ellise's grasp to continue walking toward home. He stops a dozen steps from the group and hollers at Daani, "Let's go. We have plans to make!"

Much to the chagrin of Samuel and Ellise, Cris has invited Daani into their home for a couple of days to get reacclimated to the world. Naomi takes to sleeping as close to their house as she can find accommodations in the street. That seems to satisfy her for the time being.

Samuel and Ellise would lay awake at night, listening to the two talking through all hours of the night and know they will be under their roof for a very short time. They sense the young men do not need a family roof over their heads any longer.

It comes as almost a relief when Cris and Daani rise early one morning, packed bedrolls, and some food and are gone before the cock crows. Ellise and Samuel don't even speak of their leaving as Samuel leaves for the day's work. Ellise, however, is heartbroken and weeps bitterly as she enters Cris's room and senses the emptiness.

She wonders if she will ever see Cris again. Daani would not leave without finding his mother first.

He soon discovers her sleeping spot of the previous night and approaches her quietly. As he reaches out to touch her hair, Naomi opens her eyes to look directly in Daani's face.

"I knew you would come this morning," she says softly.

Already knowing the answer, Naomi says, "Are you sure this is what you must do?"

Daani nods in response, unable to speak because of the lump in his throat. "Do you have enough clothes and food?" she asks. It is the only thing she can think to say.

Daani reaches out to touch her hair, turns on his heels, and strides away, not looking back as he matches steps with Cris. Once they reach the outskirts of Bethlehem, they head west.

Cris looks at Daani and says, "I always wanted to see what the Philistines had to offer. Ashod should be a good place to start, and besides, it's far enough away from home for us to find our own way."

If all went well, it will be about a three-day journey. The farther they get from Bethlehem, the more comfortable they become and are soon enjoying the hike and all the new things and places they pass. Their first day brings them to the outskirts of Timnah, a village smaller than Bethlehem. From a distance, they squat on their heels and discuss whether they should enter or keep their distance and travel on.

They decide to travel on and head north before turning west once again. This maneuver puts them on a direct route to the small town of Zanoah, which is about the halfway point to Ashod. Once again, they stop short of the village and contemplate their next move.

It was a good thing they had chosen to stop off the beaten path and hidden because as they were talking, a man riding in a cart being pulled by a small donkey passes by headed in the same direction. As they observe, they can't help but notice the small cart is holding a very large man. The donkey seems to labor with every step it takes and is frothing at the mouth in obvious distress. Every couple of steps by the donkey, the man bellows, "Yah! Yah!" and flicks a whip that cracks on the donkey's rear, driving it forward a few steps more.

Cris and Daani can see the bloodstains on the animal's withers from where they hid. They knew too well the sting of a whip themselves and recoil at the sound of each crack! If that isn't bad enough, they come to recognize the rider too—Cain! They can't believe it!

Seemingly, the man who was their tormenter, liar, and persecutor has followed them from Bethlehem! As they wait for the donkey, cart, and man to fade into the distance, they know they will not leave this spot until they can exact some revenge and even the score with the repulsive giant.

As far as they can figure, they need to find out two things before they make any definite plans. First, they needed to know whether Cain is going any further than Zanoah, and second, how long he plans to be there. Cris is excited about the prospect of another run-in with Cain. This time, however, they will be ready!

"The god's must be smiling down upon us, Daani! They have delivered the beast into our very hands!"

Daani isn't quite so sure that this is a good idea and offers, "We better think about this long and hard, Cris! Besides, what are you planning on doing?"

"I want to know who the little girl is and why he hurt her and why he had us whipped and put in jail. He could have made sure we were let go because he knew we didn't do anything wrong!" Cris is pretty agitated now, and Daani can see it for sure. And anyway, Daani would sure like to know about the girl too.

The sun is beginning to cast long shadows as it makes its final approach to the west. The boys guess that Cain will be stopping for the night at least, and they move back a short distance more to set up camp for the night. There will be no campfire this night. They want to make sure they remained unnoticed.

Provision

Eli wakes early every morning, and it is a routine that Jesus comes to embrace also. No matter what early time Jesus wakes, it seems Eli is already up and about. If Jesus lingers too long in his bedroll, he could count on Eli making some kind of noise or loudly singing close by to get him started. Jesus begins to wonder if Eli even sleeps.

Their days together pile one on top of the other, and Jesus cherishes each one. Eli has been given special insight into the skills and knowledge Jesus will need to start his earthly ministry. This baffles Jesus, yet, he is a diligent student and tries to grasp every word that comes from the mouth of this great old sage.

One such day, after they had spent the morning gathering wood from the surrounding area for the nighttime fire, Eli motions for Jesus to sit as they had done enough for the morning. "There. Doesn't that feel good to sit and take notice of all that you have accomplished in the morning?" Eli starts. "Did the wood gather itself or fall broken in the right size? Did it come running to the fire to be used?"

Jesus can see that this was the start of a lesson and pipes in, "It did not, teacher."

"So it is with the words that YHWH will place in your heart. You must go to the people, those you will love as the Father loves them, and gather them to your side. Gather them to sit at your feet, to learn from the words of your mouth. This will not be easy as they have long had the law of the fathers to follow and teach from. You, son, have come to them to fulfill that very law and to provide the perfect sacrifice."

"Wait, Eli!" Jesus injects. "You just said that I will fulfill the law, the law of our forefathers? And provide the perfect sacrifice? You mean like Abraham and Isaac? When YHWH provided the goat in place of Isaac? Like that?"

"Yes! Yes! That is good, Jesus! The Father will provide the only sacrifice that will ever be Sufficient when the time is right. His question to you, Jesus, is this: will you do His will when that time of sacrifice is at hand? Remember this, son, YHWH will provide the sacrifice."

Jesus answers without a pause or thought, "Of course, I will do His bidding. There is nothing I will not do for the Father!"

As soon as those words cross the lips of Jesus, the birds stop their song. The wind stops its motion. The trees stand in rapt attention. Heaven came down! The voice cries out much to the delight of the earth, "You are my Son, and I Am your Father!"

The sound of this proclamation reverberates within every object in the area. Jesus is caught off guard as is Eli, who falls face down in a cloud of dust. Jesus basks in the glory of the Father and His declaration and dares not breathe yet. He remains standing, gazing heavenward.

The event seems to last an eternity yet is over in an instant. Birds regain their song. The wind pushes the leaves, and the trees starts swaying, each refreshed and strengthened for having taken part in the splendor of that moment. They all participated in a mere moment in time that would have a consequence that even Jesus has not been given sight to see thus far.

Jesus wonders, *What kind of sacrifice YHWH will require?* And so the event of all the ages has been set in motion. All participants are in place, and the flow begins. There is no stopping it now.

The Coming Retribution

Cris and Daani wake early so as not to miss anyone coming or going from the little village. They know one of them will have to break from their hiding place to enter town and find out Cain's plans. Daani thinks he should go as he has the most experience at going unseen.

Cris agrees, and as Daani leaves their camp, he calls out, "Just find the donkey and cart. Cain won't be too far from that." Daani waves over his shoulder without looking back. He is on a mission, and he must wrap his head around the situation and remain focused. Daani jogs the quarter mile to the edge of town, and there, he slows to a walking pace.

Soon, he is mingling with other people as he walks the dusty streets trying to stay as close to the buildings as possible. As he steps off a store porch and rounds a corner, he almost runs into the backside of Cain! Luckily, Cain is facing the other way and engaged in conversation with another man. Daani nimbly backs away around the corner and breathes a sigh of relief.

As he stands there trying to regain his composure, he hears Cain say he had the goods in the cart and he wanted ten shekels for the lot. The stranger agreed to the price and follows Cain to where the donkey and cart were. Daani follows as close as he dares and is able to remain inconspicuous within hearing of their conversation.

Cain offers that as it was near to midday, he would eat before packing up and heading back to Bethlehem. "If I can get that donkey to do its job, I should be back home before dark," Cain concluded.

As Daani steals away from the encounter, he mutters to himself as he gains his stride, "We may have something to say about that,

Cain!" As Daani nears the camp spot, he slows and whistles a two note greeting to Cris already knowing he is watching the approach. Familiar notes ring back in reply, and Daani smiles to hear their familiarity.

Daani hustles the last thirty yards to where Cris is waiting, anxious to tell him all that had happened. "He's only gonna stay in town a little while longer, then he'll be heading back to Bethlehem." Daani blurts, "We can set up a spot to jump him!"

Cris has been thinking that very same thing, but he has an even better grasp of what they will do. "Let's just hope he has a lot to drink for lunch, and he'll play right into our hands."

Cris figures that Cain will have to park the donkey and get out of the cart to answer the call of nature somewhere in the trip home. They will be shadowing the procession the whole way, and that will be their chance to confront him. If they approach him while he is in the cart, he could spur the donkey on and leave them behind. They need him to be on foot.

And so with the plan formulated in their mind, they wait. It isn't long until their quarry rumbles into sight and the chase is on. They hide when they can, but also realize this road is well used, and they would be just another pair of travelers if noticed. Nonetheless, they keep their distance from Cain and cover their faces when passing others.

Their diligence is soon rewarded, and they notice the donkey veer from the road into a group of trees to the south. As providence would have it, this takes their target a good seventy-five yards from the road—perfect! They hurry to close the distance.

It is perfect timing, Cris and Daani stride up between the cart, and Cain just as he emerges from the trees and heads back toward the donkey. At the sight of the boys, Cain stops and says, "What can I do for you two?"

Then he recognizes them. "Why, look here, if it isn't the two alley rats! Fancy that we should meet again way out here in the middle of nowhere."

With that, Cris takes a step forward and points right at the monster man's face, "What did you do with the little girl in the alley? Where is she now!"

Cain chuckles. "You still hung up on that little waif? Don't you worry about her. No one will ever see her again!"

Cris and Daani look at each other with astonishment on their faces, then they both see red!

"Did you hurt her again?" Daani screams!

Cain bellows back, "She will never feel pain again, you little twit. She is none of your concern!"

"You let us get whipped and go to jail. We didn't do anything wrong!"

"You should be the one in jail!"

"You wrecked our lives!"

"Come on now, boys, you knocked me in the head and left me for dead. You got what you deserved. Besides, I thought my son should learn a real hard lesson before he got too old."

The last statement comes while Cain looks Daani right in the face, and then he sneers, baring those jagged brown teeth.

"That's right, boy. I think they call you Daani. Is that right?"

"During the trial, I couldn't help but notice your families there in attendance. While I was lookin', I thought I recognized your momma sittin' there. Of course, she didn't know who I was. I like it that way you know, knocked her in the head as I recall. She never did tell you about how you came to be, huh? Well, I remember it pretty well. Just a young street girl. With nobody to care what happened to her, she was pretty easy."

Cain was enjoying the recall and the startled look on the boys' faces when he continued, "So get out of my way, you two! I gotta get home before dark!" And then he laughed so his whole mass shook.

As the shock settles into their brains, it quickly finds its way to their fists. Fists clenched so tight that Daani already has blood flowing. His fingernails bite deep into his palms.

They advance upon their foe with blind determination to do whatever it takes to make their point. This time, they strike like lightning—one on the right and one on the left, straight at the heart of the beast.

Even with their combined weight Cain still outweighs them by a hundred pounds. This instant, however, he is caught off guard by the swiftness of their strike, and each boy gets in a couple of good punches before they are thrown to the ground. The blows don't seem to affect the giant in the least. This time, Cris goes to the front, and Daani circles to the back of their quarry.

Daani rushes his legs, and Cris chooses the direct route to Cain's head. As Daani makes contact behind the knees, Cris is flying through the air. The timing is not perfect, and Daani arrives a split second before Cris. Cain is already beginning to buckle at the knees.

Cris's flying knee makes direct contact with Cain's forehead, snapping his head back instantly. He falls to the ground with an "Umph!"

Cris and Daani both circle the fallen man. They are still full of fight with fists clenched tight. Unsure what to do next, Cris asks breathless, "You okay, Daani? That was a great move, brother!"

Daani answers, "Yeah, I'm fine. Man, that was intense!"

"Now what?" This is the question on both their minds.

They quickly go to the cart and grab the bridled donkey and lead it to the tree line. There they undo the donkey, swatting it on the rump to make it run off and push the cart deep into the trees. As they turn to head back to Cain, they make a terrifying discovery.

He is on his feet and heading right at them, enraged! He also has his massive hand wrapped around a broken tree branch the size of a forearm. Cris reacts instantly. On a dead run at their adversary, he skillfully ducks the swing of the branch and crashes into the massive midsection. Cain reaches down with his left hand and gets a handful of shirt, lifting Cris high in the air.

Cris is held suspended high over Cain's head and is mercilessly slammed back to the ground. Cris is stunned and unable to avoid the huge foot smash into his belly, pinning him down.

He vaguely remembers seeing the club poised in the air with his head as the target. The death blow never comes as Cain falls lifeless to the side. His own skull crushed by a fierce strike to the left temple. Cain is dead before he hits the ground.

Daani stands over them both with a bloody rock clenched in his hands. "Cris! Cris! you okay? Man, he was going to smash your head in!"

"I had to do it!"

"Get up! We gotta get outta here now!"

Cris wobbles to his feet and stands next to Cain's body and just stares at the motionless mass. Blood pools alongside the head, and the impact the rock made is jagged and gruesome. The dry sandy ground sops up the blood as it tries to spread. It neatly contains the spill.

A shiver runs up his spine and seems to knock him out of the daze. "Okay," Cris says, "this is what we need to do. Daani, you said he sold some stuff in the village. Let's find the money. We'll leave the body right here and bring the cart back to put alongside the body."

"Hopefully, it'll look like he got robbed and killed by those groups of roving thieves and robbers. Nobody would believe it was us. Besides, if we run all night, we can be in Ashod by the morning and have a pretty good alibi. And by the way, Daani, thanks for saving me. He would have killed me for sure."

Daani still has the rock in his hands and looks up from staring at it. "Yeah, sounds like a plan to me, Cris. We'd better get moving, though."

He drops the bloody rock next to the inert figure. They run to the hidden cart and pull it back next to Cain's body. Rifled through Cain's belongings until they find the ten shekels in a pouch and Cris ties it to his belt. Then they run like the wind, heading west and shadowing the road as best they can, at least until the sun sets.

They both believe with all their hearts they can start over in Ashod. Now they just need to get there as fast as possible.

In Darkness

Eli encouraged Jesus on a regular basis to leave their little camp and be on his own for a couple of days or weeks. Jesus would oblige by packing his stuff and setting off for parts unknown. Every time that Jesus left, Eli would call after him saying, "The Lord your God is with you, He is mighty to save. He will take great delight in you with His love. He will rejoice over you with singing." (Zeph. 3:17).

Jesus looked forward to hearing Eli quote this old scripture, nearly as much as he looked forward to his time spent in the wilderness alone. It always brought a smile to his face and lifted his spirit.

One such sashay into the unknown brought Jesus face-to-face with one of the toughest challenges of his young life. Jesus found an oasis out in the middle of nowhere, and it seemed to be the perfect spot for an extended stay. It had everything a wanderer could ask for. There were enough trees for shade and fuel and plenty of cool fresh water from a spring emerging from a pile of rocks. Jesus was sure there would be a steady stream of birds and animals stopping by and was confident of his skills with the sling now.

This is going to be great! Jesus had always carried the scriptures in his possessions and thought this would be a perfect time of reading, study, and prayer. The first night, as Jesus cuddled up to the fire and his bedroll, he was reading from the book of beginnings, Genesis. As he read and considered the teachings, he noticed his eyesight growing dim and thought it was the fire going out and took it as a sign to turn in for the night.

His sleep was full of unrest and visions of darkness. And darkness was what Jesus woke to the next morning. As he stirred, he was sure it was after sun up as he could hear birds singing. Yet with eyes wide open, he could register no light at all. *This is strange,* Jesus thought. *Is it a day without light?*

Then it came to him; he is blind! He stood from his bed and tried vainly to remember exactly where he had laid down last night. How far from the fire? How far from the trees? Which way was the spring? And then finally, why?

The realization slowly crept over him that this was a test he would have to figure out all by himself. Jesus plopped back down to the ground and sat there to think. "Okay," he says to himself, "you just spent day after day with a blind man, what have you learned and what can you remember?"

First things first! He realizes he must determine his surroundings and file them in his memory. Jesus slowly begins feeling around and bumping into this and that. He finally finds all his belongings and gathers them all together in one spot. This is very frustrating! He struggles mightily and doesn't seem to be doing very well.

Then it comes to him; he is struggling with his loss of a sense and not concentrating on the senses he still has. *Slow down, take a deep breath, and listen, feel, and savor.* And finally he recognizes another important matter that he has neglected!

Jesus falls to his knees and calls out to YHWH, "Father, hear me! If it weren't for Your plan, I would be undone. Give me wisdom, and let me understand Your will in this lesson. Amen." Jesus feels completely renewed and invigorated. His inner vision is restored, and now he understands the purpose of this blindness.

This new awareness doesn't seem to help his physical limitation though, and he soon resorts to hand wringing and worry. It paralyses him once again.

Ashod Ahead

The duo makes it to Ashod in good time, and just as they had envisioned, they arrive near sun up the next day. The town beckons to them as they enter the city outskirts. It was so busy!

They smile at each other, and Cris says, "I think we can blend in here just fine! Nobody will even notice us. There are so many people!"

Daani couldn't wipe the smile off his face as they walked into the morning hustle and bustle. Within minutes they had become lost in the sea of people and noise. As luck would have it, Cris and Daani entered through the east gate, and they became immersed in the marketplace. They could not believe all the things for sale and for trade! There were fruits and animals and vegetables they had never even seen before. All sorts of woven goods and leather and brightly colored shirts and tunics, sandals of all kinds, and carts and wagons filled to the overflowing with stuff!

Man, what a sight! The sound was something they could not have imagined either. Cattle and sheep and poultry of all sorts, monkeys and goats—all making a wonderful, mixed-up clatter that vibrated into their core.

And the people! All kinds of shapes and sizes, differently dressed, and speaking in tongues they could not understand. Some men wore great swords and others with clubs and bows and arrows. Wow! And soldiers here and there with some type of armor and helmets, and the women!

Cris and Daani could not help but notice the beautiful women scattered amongst the crowded streets. Most women had their faces covered, but others openly displayed fine features and smooth dark skin and haunting eager eyes. Those eyes!

They caught themselves staring on more than one occasion, and they would quickly divert their faces when the women looked their way. Their blush ran all the way to their hearts! The wonders of Ashod! And they have only walked one street! Both were exhausted from their all-night trek, and they really needed to sit and get something to eat.

They looked around and saw a likely looking inn with a porch that jutted into the street. Cris elbows Daani and points toward the porch and declares, "Let's go over there!"

Without waiting for an answer, he starts cutting through the crowd, expecting Daani to follow, and follow he did. Neither Cris nor Daani had never been in a public eating place and really didn't know what to do or how to act. They sat at a table like others who were there. They were talking in a low voice when a man dressed in soiled clothes with a clean apron tied about his waist approached their table.

The man looked at them both and inquired, "What brings you two to my establishment? Are you men new in town?"

Cris jumped quickly on the query and says, "We've been in town since yesterday, just looking for something to eat and drink right now."

The man eyed them both quickly and asked, "You got money?"

Cris again answers, saying, "Sure we do!"

"Okay, okay!" The proprietor says, "Just checking, that's all. What would you like?" Without waiting for an answer, he adds, "We got fresh bread and good wine. It'll be one denarii each."

Cris looked at Daani and shakes his head and says out loud, "That's good. We'll have that." As the man turns to walk away, Cris reaches out and grabs his hand, causing the man to stop and look back. Cris continues, "All we have is shekels to pay with."

The man responds, "Those work just fine. It'll be one half shekel then."

The man turned on his heel and walked briskly away from their table, disappearing through a doorway to the back.

Whew, Cris thought, *glad to have that out of the way.*

Daani finally speaks and says, "Nice job, Cris. I was kinda at a loss for words. Bread and wine will be great!"

Cris answers, "It sure will, but that is a lot of money for bread and wine. We'll have to be more careful about what we buy from now on. We have to make the money last."

Shortly, the man arrived back at their table with a fresh loaf of bread and a leather container of wine and two earthen cups. He sets the entire contents down and stands with his hand out to Cris. Cris dutifully recovers the pouch from his belt and dumps the ten shekels out on the table, picks out one, and hands it to the man who hands back to Cris a shekel neatly cut in half. Cris scoops the rest of the coins into his hand and deposits them back into the pouch and ties it to his belt once again.

The twosome eagerly divided the loaf in half and fill the cups; the feast is on! And did it ever taste good! They eat with their heads down and didn't pay attention to the others in the inn. But just about the time they were going to finish off the entire loaf of bread, Daani looks up and grabs Cris and says, "We need to save some of the bread. Wrap it up for later."

"Yeah, good idea, Daani, you never know when we might need it." With that, they each wrap the heel of the loaf in their food pouch. There, now at least they have something for later. As they begin to get up from the table, the inn man approaches them once again.

"Are you two looking for a place to stay the night?"

"I've got a room with a spot for you to throw your bedrolls down and sleep. You'll be sharing it with a couple others, though."

"How much?" Cris asks.

"Well, since you two already spent some money at my inn here," the man says, "I'll let you both stay for one denarii a night. Gotta pay in advance though, and you know you'll have a roof over your head and a bowl full of water to wash up. You can come and go as you please."

"Me and my partner will think about it and let you know by midday. That Okay with you?" Cris asks.

"Sure is. I'll be here. By the way, my name is Benaiah. You can call me Ben. Everybody in town knows me." They leave the inn and head back into the crowd of people, refreshed and full and already with a new friend.

Daani looks at Cris and exclaims, "Man, I'm already liking Ashod!"

New Sight

Jesus spends seven days in his newfound condition of blindness. He goes without food, a fire, and vainly fumbles around his campsite, fearing getting too far away to return to his belongings. His humanness has paralyzed his divinity. How do others do it?

He cries out in human frustration, "Father! You have given me too much to bear! How can I learn at Your feet if I cannot survive?" An unnerving silence follows. And then suddenly, Jesus can feel the authority of the light through his darkened eyes and knows the presence is with him.

He shudders as the voice speaks, "Listen, my Son, and be still!" The last word reverberated, rumbling across the ground, soaring to the heavens unabated. The whole earth dared not make a sound as the rumblings faded into the distance.

"Do you not feel it? Do you not understand what courses through your being? You are heaven come down to earth, and what you say here shapes eternity. You need only bear these tests for as long as you desire, to better know those whom you will love, as I love you. I have sent you to be all things through Me, to all those you will gather to yourself. You will cause the blind to see, the lame to walk, the deaf to hear, the dead to breathe again. You are the Redeemer! Speak, and it will be!"

Jesus could not speak. He could not believe or fully understand what YHWH had just revealed.

During this enlightenment, Jesus has instinctively covered his head with both hands and hid his face from the Almighty. The last words were still echoing in his mind as he dares to uncover his head.

Revealing that his hands are as white as snow, he can only imagine what his face looks like! Then it struck him; his sight was restored, and his vision is so clear he can see for miles and miles! As he stares at his hands, he can think of only one thing to speak, "Thank You, Father!"

He looks heavenward just in time to see the firmament closing around brilliant white raiment disappearing into the sky. "Yes! Indeed!" Jesus proclaims. Jesus could contain himself no longer. He must get back to Eli and ask for his help in fully understanding what has just taken place. He gathers his belongings in haste, bundles them together, and sets off on a dead run back the way he had traveled. He runs for hours and is exhausted when finally he arrives back at the camp that he and Eli share.

"Eli, Eli!" Jesus calls out. But there is no answer. Jesus once again searches with his voice, "Eli, I need you!"

Then faintly, way off in the distance, Jesus hears a sound. *What is that? A cry for help? A groan? What?* Jesus focuses on the direction of the sound and sees the very same rocky outcropping he had passed through when he first found Eli's camp. He was sure the sound had come from there. He didn't waste any time getting there. As he slowed to a trot on his approach, he calls out once again, "Eli! Eli!" And he hears the sound again, this time much closer and louder.

Jesus picks his way up the rocks and boulders. He hears the sound again, and this time, it is accompanied by the unmistakable sound of a deep growl! He jumps from rock to rock with newfound vigor. As Jesus reaches the source of the sounds, he is shocked to see Eli! He sits slumped over with his back to a large boulder, and circling directly in front of him is a huge lion! As Jesus looks more closely at Eli, he sees blood from a wound to his head and detects no movement coming from his mentor!

Quickly, Jesus whispers, "Father, help me!" and he steps into the open. The lion instantly loses focus on the old man and sees nothing else but Jesus. Jesus intuitively stretches forth his hand toward the lion and moves to put himself between the two.

Jesus recalls the intensity and malice in the yellow eyes of the first lion he ever came this close too, and he sees it once again. He is bolder this time, however, and continues walking calmly toward the beast.

With each step Jesus advances, the lion's ferocity lessens. Its bared teeth become covered. He relaxes the taunt muscles of his legs and back and slowly sinks into a prone position. And finally, as Jesus reaches the adversary, the lion seemingly gives up and lays his massive head on its front legs.

Jesus calmly speaks to the brute, "You can go now. You are no longer needed." As the words come from the mouth of Jesus, the lion stands, stretches, shakes vigorously, and slowly pads away.

Jesus quickly turns his attention to Eli and puts his ear to the bony chest, listening for a heartbeat. There was one! Faint at best. Jesus gathers Eli into his arms and turns to leave and, in so doing, causes a flock of vultures to take to the air, their raspy calls cursing in disgust as the warm air fills their huge wings. They soar away.

Jesus shudders at the thought of what was just averted and once again wonders at the provision of the Almighty! He can't wait to hear Eli's version of what had taken place. He hustles the limp form of Eli back to their camp and begins nursing him back to health and attending to his needs and wounds. Jesus's complete focus is on Eli, and he immerses himself in that undertaking.

Jesus will not leave Eli's side for three days. On the third day, Jesus finally notices a little color returning to Eli's gaunt face. Jesus has been trying to force liquids into his patient the entire time, and at last, he can see some results. It isn't long until Eli sits up and opens his lifeless eyes, looking about but not seeing. "My son ,where are we? Have I returned to the presence of the Almighty?" he asks.

Now it is Jesus's turn to chuckle as he touches Eli's arm and assures him, "You are earthbound just as I am. And when you are better, you will have some explaining to do."

Eli turns in Jesus direction and offers, "I do, do I? Well, what do I have to explain to you?"

So Jesus counters, "How did you get that far away from camp, and Why would you wander that far away?"

"After you left and were gone for a couple of days, I decided I needed a change of scenery!" Eli offered. They both smiled at that!

"And besides, what possibly could happen to an old blind man wandering alone in the desert?"

Jesus couldn't help but laugh out loud now! "I was doing fine until I came to that rocky part where you found me. I didn't really know how big it was, but I was determined to get to the top of it. And climb I did! By the way, Jesus, did I make it to the top?" Eli asks.

Jesus is obligated to answer, "Yes, you made it pretty close to the top. Now go on!"

"Okay, okay," Eli continues. "It had to be just about where you found me. I kind of lost my footing and fell pretty hard and must have hit my head. I remember waking up and was all scrunched up in some big rocks and could feel the blood running down my head, and I can't seem to move. Right away, I think, Jesus will be mad at me about this!"

He continues, "I also hear the sound of animals all around me, like birds, big birds! They are scratching and cawing, and finally, I feel them on me! They start pecking and clawing at my clothes and my skin! And did I tell you I can't move? I'm starting to think that this isn't going to end well and think that YHWH just might be calling me home. Just about that time I hear this noise, like something else is coming near me walking up the rocks and boulders. Except, this was different that a person walking, more like an animal of some kind. And the birds, they all stop their tearing at me and scatter. Then I hear this low growl from a big hairy beast. Within seconds, I feel the warm breath and smell the putrid stench of rotten meat— not good! And did I tell you I can't move?

"This creature opens its mouth wide and grabs me around the chest! I feel the huge teeth press up against my skin and just wait for the final crunch of my bones breaking. It never comes as the beast gently lifts me from the rocks, turns, and makes its way down to a sandy flat spot. It lays me down next to a big rock and becomes my guardian! I can hear it pacing back and forth, and every once in a while, it utters a low growl, not directed at me but at something!"

"Can you believe it, Jesus? The hand of the Almighty sent the king of beasts to watch over me until you came and found me! I vaguely remember the sound of you approaching and talking to the lion. What did you say to it?"

Jesus has been mesmerized by the account of the amazing guardian the Almighty provided and offers, "I simply told him he was no longer needed, and he left."

"Wow, what a story, and what provision by the Father!" With that, Eli suddenly feels the drain on his human body and drifts off in welcome sleep lying on his side. Jesus puts some clothes under his head and covers his frail old body with a warm skin.

Jesus softly says to the sleeping prophet, "Eli, I really have some amazing things to tell you too! I need your help filling in some blanks. That is, when you are fully rested and recovered." Jesus can't wait to tell Eli of his own wilderness experiences.

Ashod's Allure

As Cris and Daani are immersed once again in this alien culture, they marvel at every turn at the diversity and sensory stimulation they receive. The wandering finally brings them to the center of Ashod and a whole new insight into Philistine customs. There stands a temple that is obviously the heart of activity and hub of worship.

They soon find out that it is the temple of Dagon, one of the many gods of this people. The temple is surrounded by all sorts of small booths containing items of sacrifice used for entry into the temple. The booth operators are also hawkers, shouting loudly at every passersby, proclaiming the virtues of their goods for sale.

One booth is more opulent than the others and a little different. The proprietor is a comely woman, in bright dress and bare face. As the young men walk by, she addresses them personally, "Good day to be in Ashod wouldn't you say? Would you care to look at my goods for sale for access into the temple of Dagon? Come, come, boys. I promise I won't bite!"

Cris was instantly taken by the beauty and boldness of this siren, while Daani could sense it would not be good to engage her. Cris, therefore, was the first to succumb to the invitation and stopped to face the woman. Daani continued on a couple more steps and stopped to motion for Cris to follow, but his focus was solely on the woman.

Seeing the futility of continuing, Daani turned and sided up to Cris. Daani tried to avert his eyes but soon found himself completely immersed in her allure also. The woman had a dark complexion, with high cheekbones and smooth skin. Her dark hair is gathered loosely atop her head, exposing her neck. Her hair is held in place by ivory pins. Big golden earrings hang jangling from her pierced ears, and she wears a soft, tanned leather dress, tied about the waist with a scarlet sash. The dress is adorned with brightly colored beads and leather fronds hanging from the neck, sleeves, and hem. She carries herself with a confident air that the young men were not accustomed to seeing in a woman.

And they certainly weren't used to being this close to such a beautiful woman at that! It didn't take long for the woman to figure out she has the upper hand in this dalliance, and she plans on using it to her advantage. "You young men see anything you like?" She asks, smiling and placing her hands on her hips.

"My name is Sheba by the way. By what names do you go by, may I ask?" She looks first at Cris and then at Daani, pausing long enough for each to offer their names in response. The two responded with their names.

"Well, Cris and Daani, what brings you two to the glorious city of Ashod this fine day?" Planning on staying in control of the conversation, Sheba continues without pause, "Where are you from, and how long do you plan on staying in Ashod?"

Without thinking, Daani speaks, "We are from Bethlehem and just want to see what the big city has to offer."

"Well, well, we have us a couple of Hebrew men here, don't we? Your kind tend to stay away from Ashod and keep to your own, but hey, I'm glad you are here! Where did you say you were staying while you are in town?" Sheba countered.

Cris picks up the conversation now and offers, "We are staying over at an inn by the east gate for now. A guy named Ben runs it. We're just kind of finding our way around town today and seeing what is here."

"Well, boys, I'm usually here every day until midday or past. If you need anything, just stop by, and I'll point you in the right direction." With that, Sheba turns her attention abruptly from the boys and returns to selling her wares.

Cris and Daani are kind of just left standing there with their mouths hanging open. They turn to leave, and Sheba calls after them, "You two are welcome in my shop anytime you wish."

"Man, that is one pretty woman," Cris says as they walk away.

Daani continues that thought with, "Yeah, and she knows it too!"

"Yeah, I agree with you on that one, friend," Cris says. "I don't think I'll forget her for as long as I live. She stole my heart!" he says as he fakes fainting.

Daani pokes Cris in the ribs and says, "Well, as long as that is all she steals, you'll be okay!" They both laugh as they walk away.

Then Cris remembers something he said back at the temple and offers, "We'd better get back to Ben's and pay for the room for a couple of nights and stash our bedrolls so we can check out the city some more. What do you say, Daani?"

"Yep, that sounds good to me. Let's go."

Daani and Cris begin heading back toward the east gate and the inn with the proprietor named Ben. The big city is a new and frightening thing for them, and they stick close together. The crowded street presents an intimidating gauntlet, and they are relieved when the familiar-looking porch comes in view. The young men waste no time finding Ben and securing a sleeping spot for the next couple of days. Ben shows them the room and helps them stash their bedrolls.

As Ben turns to leave, he calls over his shoulder a warning, a reminder, "Don't leave anything unguarded that you want to keep 'cause it won't be there in the morning!" With that, he is through the door and back to business.

Cris and Daani eye each other, and Cris says, "You want me to carry all the stuff we can't afford to lose?"

Daani nods his head affirmatively and offers, "You think our bedrolls will be okay?"

Cris laughs and says, "Man, you had a whiff of them lately? They are almost as bad as our clothes!"

Daani laughs too and says, "Yeah, we should find a place to have our stuff washed tomorrow or find a place we can do it ourselves at least."

"That's a great idea for tomorrow. Right now, we are going to check out what happens around here when the sun goes down!" With all their "valuables" strapped to their waists under their clothes, they head into the unknown world of Ashod at night.

If the lads thought the daylight presented some amazing sights, they were really in for a treat now.

Back home, when the sun went down, pretty much everyone turned in and attended to family gatherings and dinner. Here, it was completely different. Cris and Daani wondered if anybody was at home!

The streets and porches and alleys and sidewalks are packed with people. And what people! Costumes and masks and bright clothes and dark clothes and face paint! Man alive, was this place hopping! There are flute players and harps and drummers and stringed instruments they had never seen before and men and women motioning for them to come over.

Daani pokes Cris in the ribs and motions toward a woman standing by the corner of a building. She is looking directly at them, waving for them to come. Daani says half-joking, "What do you suppose she wants, Cris? Think she knows we have some money?"

Cris says, "Don't even think about it. Nobody knows unless we tell 'em!"

"Let's just keep moving. I'd like to get a real good picture of the lay of the land tonight so we can plan the next couple of days and maybe look for some work," says Cris as he moves on.

Daani is a step behind and pauses one last time to look at the woman on the corner. He shakes his head in disbelief as he walks away, muttering under his breath, "What a place!"

They walk for another hour just taking in the sights and filling their heads with wonder. They come to a corner, and Cris stops and looks at Daani. "Okay, buddy, which way? Left or right? You choose."

Daani eyes both ways for a few seconds and then says, "To the left, to adventure!"

They laugh, and off they go. They haven't travelled more than a few minutes when right before them stands a beautiful woman with a see-through veil covering the lower portion of her face. Just her eyes are showing. She is dressed in an exquisitely adorned purple dress. Gold rings gilded her wrists and neck, and silver beads hang on silk thread woven into her shiny black hair. She has a certain familiarity about her, but the guys are startled when she utters, "Well, hello there, Cris and Daani. I didn't expect to see you again so soon."

It is Sheba! They about had a heart attack to say the least! "Is that really you, Sheba?" exclaimed Cris. "Geez, you scared the daylights out of me!"

"And me too!" Daani mimed.

Cris continued, "I am sorry, but I didn't recognize you. You are beautiful! I mean, well, well, you know what I mean!"

Sheba starts to smile and laugh at these two in front of her. She takes complete control of the awkwardness and reaches out and hooks both of their arms with hers and centers herself between them. Sheba calmly says, "How about I show you two around our fantastic city. You know, a guided tour!"

The duo surely had never envisioned their first night in Ashod to be like this! It is a dream come true!

No one back home would ever believe they were being shown the city at night, on the arm of the most beautiful woman in town. You could see their smiles from a block away.

As the night wears on and Sheba introduces them to more and more of her acquaintances, they cannot believe their good fortune! They are meeting everyone in town. This just has to be a good way to start a new life!

The trio turns a last corner, and Ben's inn comes in sight. Sheba says, "Well, boys, I believe this is where we part company for the night."

To tell the truth, Cris and Daani were exhausted, and the thought of their own bedroll was very enticing right now. However, Daani could not let this opportunity go by without offering, "Will you be okay walking back by yourself? We will be glad to escort you back safely."

"Oh, how nice of you to offer," Sheba says coyly, "but I am completely safe, and besides there are more people I want to see before I turn in, but it is very sweet of you to offer! Good night!"

She walks away, and the boys cannot take their eyes off her! A few yards out, she turns back around and knowingly catches them staring after her. She calls out, "And by the way, I want to see you both tomorrow before noonday!" With that, she vanishes. The night swallows her like some exquisite otherworldly apparition.

The sounds of the evening bring them out of their momentary enchantment. And finally, they seek out the comfort of their bed-roll and a quiet respite. Although tired beyond description, Cris and Daani can hardly sleep thinking about their being with Sheba this night and their meeting the next day!

At the first hint of dawn, they are up and locate Ben to find out where they might wash their clothes and clean up a bit. Ben was very interested in their first night and the fact they were escorted by Sheba.

"Wow, I'm impressed, guys. Sheba is one powerful woman in Ashod. She knows everyone and is highly respected for her various skills!" At that, Ben winks at them both. "And besides all that, she is very easy on the eyes! Right, boys?" He winks again while flashing a devilish smile. "I understand why you want to get cleaned up! And I know just where to send you."

Cris and Daani hurry to their meeting with Sheba. They can't believe how good they feel in clean clothes and clean bodies. They are looking good! But they can't help but wonder what Sheba would want with them!

Daani pipes up as they walk, "What do you suppose Sheba wants with us today?"

Cris answers, smiling, "I really could care less what she wants as long as we get to see her again!"

Daani wags his head in disbelief, smiles, and offers, "Man, you got it bad!"

And they pick up the pace. Sheba smiles to herself as the two come into her view. As soon as they look in her direction, she waves and gets the expected response. Both Cris and Daani wave enthusiastically. Sheba doesn't wait for the boys to reach her booth totally, but knowing they are watching, she waves. "Follow me," she says and vanishes behind the back curtain, leaving the booth momentarily empty.

Both young men see the overt gesture and enter the booth without breaking stride. They duck behind the same curtain. Out of the daylight and without any source of light, they stop just inside the enclosure to let their eyes adjust and strain to see what lay in front of them. When finally their eyes adjust, they find themselves in a tent corridor that attaches to the outside wall of the temple of Dagon!

And to top that, Sheba is nowhere in sight! The guys are flabbergasted! They know for sure Sheba came this way, and straight ahead looks like a solid wall. They edge forward not knowing what to expect. As they get to within ten feet of the wall, a sliver of light appears. The nearer they get, the larger the sliver becomes until they reach the wall and see the light comes from a doorway of sorts. Part of the wall is obviously pivoting somehow, so Cris reaches out and pushes against the side where the light is. The wall moves silently out of the way, revealing the dimly lit interior of a good-sized room!

"What the?" Cris exclaims as he shields Daani from an unknown, unseen menace.

Slowly, Cris peers into the room, and his tensed muscles suddenly relax as he utters a nervous laugh of relief. He spies Sheba on the other side of the room and figures all is well.

Over his shoulder, Cris offers, "It's okay. She's here. Let's go."

They enter the chamber in the side of the temple of Dagon. They head directly for the only familiar thing in the room—Sheba. The room is lit with hundreds of candles and oil lamps scattered about, each one casting an eerie shadow on walls and other objects in attendance.

And what objects they are, all sorts of statues and goblets and lavers. Some statues are gilded and others are not. Some large and some small, but they all seem to be of the same thing. That being a man's torso with a fish type lower body. This thing just had to be the object of the temple.

Perhaps Dagon himself! And then there was Sheba! She reclines on a pile of soft furs and smiles at them as they approach. "So glad you could make it, Cris and Daani, I was hoping you hadn't forgotten about my invitation."

Daani pipes up, "We could hardly wait to see you again, but what are we doing in here?"

Sheba motions for them to come closer and to sit down on the floor. She reclines at just about eye level to the sitting lads. "I thought you would like to see the inside of the temple, and besides, it is so much cooler in here than outside."

That it was, but in the boys eyes, it was warming quickly! Sheba has the entirety of their attention as she begins, "I could really use the services of a couple of strong young men such as you two. How would you like to help me out with some ongoing projects that I am involved in? You would work for me when I need you, and I would provide you with a clean place to bed and money as needed for things. I would expect you to be available to me whenever I need you. You would be responsible to me and me alone. And oh, I need to be able to trust you completely. Our relationship will be perfect as long as I can trust you!"

The young men cannot take their eyes off Sheba as she outlines her proposal. Their hearts tell them they should run, but the animal instinct in them both says yes! Cris blurts out, "This sounds like a perfect opportunity for us to be a part of the life of Ashod." And without even looking at Daani, he says, "We'll do it!"

Sheba exclaims, "This is wonderful! I think we will have a great relationship, and good for all of us. Now, how long are you staying at Ben's inn? I need you to stay there for at least a few more days so I can arrange a couple of different places for you to stay. Besides, it'll give you a chance to work the nights some more and find your own way around."

"What do you say?" This, of course, was a mute question.

That first night and next day turned into hundreds and hundreds more just like it. Cris and Daani soon become a fixture in Ashod's nightlife. The first couple of nights at Ben's inn led to a series of moves from inn to inn, and with the guidance of Sheba, they soon found work and always had a place to stay, just like she had promised.

The young men quickly become men and a force to be reckoned with on the streets. They were never without each other and took to their new position in life like they were born for it. Where Cris was, Daani was, and where Daani was, Cris was. They were inseparable.

Cris and Daani have arrived. Daani and Cris deepened their trust in Sheba and were regular visitors to the temple of Dagon. Their early life teachings of the scriptures and the ways of the Hebrew people were but a glimmer in their memories now. Their muscles and minds hardened at the daily and nightly exposure to Ashod's underbelly. They became creatures of their environment and completely lost their sense of a moral compass. They eagerly did Sheba's bidding and became her willing slaves of perversion.

Eli's Sight

The fifth day after Eli's rescue and return to camp, he is up and about as usual, feeling his way around. As he hums a tune in his raspy voice, he purposely bumps into Jesus as he squatted to tend the fire. The bump nearly knocks Jesus over, and Jesus hollers, "Hey! Watch where you're going!"

Eli laughs out loud and exclaims, "Yeah, like that's going to happen!"

They both laugh and laugh until they collapse. Jesus looks at this old sage as they calm down and marvels at God's wisdom in providing this man for his tutor. Jesus thinks this might be the perfect time for him to share what had taken place on his last trip into the wilderness and hopefully get some answers too.

"Eli, I am perplexed by what my Father proffered at our last meeting in the wilderness," Jesus states.

"Tell me," Eli says, "what has you so concerned, son."

"Well, I guess the best thing would be to start at the beginning and let you offer some insight."

"Yes, yes, of course, begin!" Eli takes a deep breath and crosses his legs, preparing for a sitting of epoch proportions.

"I was struck with blindness for seven days, and I don't think I handled it very well. It proved to be one of the most difficult challenges I have ever faced. I felt so alone and helpless. I could do nothing!" Jesus lamented as he was taken back to vivid recall.

Eli is very surprised at this revelation and offers, "I am not surprised that YHWH chose blindness for you to experience. It certainly is a perfect example of the darkness that many people encounter every day in their lives, both physically and spiritually. How did you overcome this trial?"

At that question, Jesus felt ashamed and knew exactly where this was going. "I didn't solve anything! In fact, I was overpowered by fear!"

"Jesus, you already know the answer. I want you to listen to what you have just stated and tell me the answer."

Jesus' response does not surprise Eli, "I tried in my own power to fix the problem and could not. My Father was there, waiting for me to come to Him for insight and answers, and I tried on my own and failed miserably. How could I be so shortsighted?" Jesus wags his head in disgust with himself. "I gave up, before I sought His will."

"All is not lost, my son, you have had time to reflect on your actions and now must learn and move on. There will be more of these experiences, these physical tests for you to learn from. And that is what you must do, learn and move on." Eli is eager to get to the real crux of this conversation as the Almighty has given him vision of what is to come this day. "What else was revealed to you that you do not understand, my son? I am curious to hear how you perceived what happened in your meeting with YHWH."

So Jesus continues, "The Almighty appeared to me while I was still in the state of blindness, but I know He was there, and it was awesome! He spoke to me and told of marvelous feats I would do and great gifts I would have through Him."

"You simply must accept the position YHWH has given you upon this earth. But I will tell you this: the Father has given me the authority to reveal to you these things. When you can say these words and they make sense to you, you will fully understand your purpose. Remember them well, Jesus, Son of the Most High!"

Eli pauses to gather his thoughts and shudders at the enormity of what he is about to tell this young man before him. "This is what you must say, 'I and the Father are One!' When you are able to say these words, you will also be able to accept all the responsibility and power the Father will accord you while on earth. This means that what you bind together on earth will be bound together in heaven. What you loose on earth will be loosed in heaven. You will be given power over land and sea, and they too will do your bidding. Death and sickness and suffering will hold no sway over you. Demons will flee at the mention of your name. Eternity has been placed in your heart, and you will save all those that believe your Word. Your final act on this earth will give everyone hope through your victory over death and the grave. Now, Jesus, I want you to listen carefully. All these endowments come at a price, a redemptive price. And there is only One that can provide the sacrifice the Father requires for the redemption of humanity.

"Jesus, the Great I Am has sent you to be life eternal to all those who accept you. You, Jesus, are the perfect sacrifice!"

Jesus knew this revelation would come but underestimated the power it would have when he heard the truth spoken!

And Eli wasn't finished yet! "You will suffer mightily at the hands of those that will not accept you or your word. You will be physically broken, and your blood will be offered as the sacrifice for all those called by your name. The Father has ordained that you will be lifted up between the balance of the firmament and heaven, and your life's blood be emptied upon this sod. You must submit to this willingly and agree to the Father's plan."

Jesus falls to his knees and lifts his eyes and hands toward heaven. This voice cannot be contained in his body any longer, and he breaks forth, proclaiming, "I and the Father are One! Your will be done on earth as it is in heaven!"

Eli's Joy, Jesus's Loss

Eli stops because he is drained of all strength. The consequence of what he has spoken will soon lead to his return to the Father. Now that Jesus has realized his ultimate purpose on earth, Eli too is facing an ultimate happening. He knows his time on earth with Jesus is drawing to an end, and his heart is heavy with that realization.

Eli has not only cared for and loved Jesus, but he has been instrumental in Jesus attaining the *full* awareness of his heavenly gifts and earthly purpose and his godly lineage. Eli knew from the beginning his own purpose, but what he hadn't planned on was becoming so attached to his pupil. Eli feels no disrespect in calling Jesus his son as he truly has cherished these past four years. Has it indeed been that long? It seems like only yesterday this young man came stumbling into his camp by God's design. And their connection began in the twinkling of an eye—YHWH's eye.

The days and nights filled with talking, teaching, and laughter, which are vividly etched in his mind's eye and even now cause a smile to cross his lips and a tear to form. Oh, how he will miss the closeness and Jesus's constant yearning for knowledge and the yearning for his destiny to be revealed.

Eli wonders whether there has ever been a relationship like this on earth before or if there will ever be again. He has done the Father's bidding and has seen his scholarship rewarded in the fullness of Jesus's earthly completion.

Oh, Jesus looks the same on the outside, although now there is an air about him that makes you want to be in his presence. But Eli knows now the fullness of the godhead that resides on the inside—

the completed work. It is humbling to have been entrusted with a charge that all heaven has been a part of designing.

Eli has come to the end of his second earthly term, and it does not seem forward in asking one more thing of the Creator before he leaves. Eli falls prostrate and breathlessly whispers, "My Master and Maker, hear me now I cry. You have blessed me beyond measure as a part of the plan for Your Son, Jesus. I have done Your bidding. Grant me now I pray one last longing of this servant's heart before I return to Your glory! Oh, Father, that I may see Jesus!"

Eli could feel the answer as the Father granted this request and placed in Eli's heart these words, "My Son will see to it!"

Eli cries out with great joy in his voice! "Jesus! I want to see You!" and rises to his knees.

Jesus is still in his own state of worship, yet he senses an urgency in Eli's voice he had never heard before. Rushing to Eli's side, Jesus kneels before him, taking his old weathered hand in his own. "I am here, friend."

Eli knows this will be the end of their earthly relationship. This one last act of love. He stutters, "Jesus, son, the Father has allowed me one last request that is to be fulfilled by your hand." Eli weeps as he says, "I desire to see you face-to-face."

Jesus is deeply moved by this request and trembles as he releases the hold on Eli's hand and places his hands on Eli's frail, narrow shoulders. Jesus leans forward, placing his cheek upon the leathery cheek of Eli and whispers into his ear, "You are loved!"

In an instant, the once dead eyes of Eli dance to life! Eli quickly shuts them tight and pushes Jesus back away from himself. Only when he has Jesus at arm's length does he reopen his eyes! And what a sight he sees! Jesus face-to-face! "Today, I have seen the Savior! I am complete!" Eli cries in great exultation!

Jesus's elation at the light shining forth from the face of his friend and mentor is quickly dimmed. For as soon as Eli completes his testimony, the light fades and is snuffed out from Eli's human being. Jesus catches the slumping form of his beloved teacher and pulls his frail shell to his chest. Eli is earthbound no more. Joy turns to anguish in a heartbeat! And Jesus' s heart breaks, and tears flow as he slowly rocks back and forth.

Jesus clings to Eli's body until the warmth begins to fade. He doesn't ask why because he knows. The human emptiness is a new experience, feelings he must endure and learn from. Even in departing, his beloved friend provided one last lesson, and Jesus is thankful for that. Jesus lovingly carries Eli's body to the edge of the campsite they have called home for these many years and eases him down. He gathers rocks to cover the body. He turns and walks back to find some items that he will place with the body before burial.

As he is in the midst of going through Eli's meager earthly possessions, a brilliant flash of light engulfs the area, startling Jesus in its intensity. He turns to see the place where Eli was laid containing only his clothing. His body is gone! Jesus smiles at the finality of this resurrection! Amen!

Homeward

Jesus moped around the campsite for a couple of days. The loss of the physical presence of Eli weighs greatly upon his soul. All he has to do is close his eyes, and the vivid recollections of Eli are instantly present. But he has a hole in his heart that cannot be filled with solitude, or lessons learned, or memories.

Jesus knows without a doubt exactly where Eli is at this very moment. He must take solace in the promise of the Almighty, and he feels these words riding the afternoon breeze, "So you will know the depth of My love for you, even now you must know the sorrow of love lost only for a moment! Do not grieve, My Son, like the rest of men that have no hope for You are the great hope giver!"

Once again, Jesus understands and wipes a solitary tear from his eye. He knows he will leave this place, never to return. Jesus gathers his belongings and takes a step. Jesus knows the path to Nazareth goes both ways. He is sure he would be welcomed home, if he chose to return. For now, he will choose to begin heading that way and see what the Almighty will bring across his path. At the thought of home, Jesus smiles then turns and heads westward in the general direction of Nazareth.

He can't remember how many miles or days from Nazareth he had travelled when first he found Eli. Of course, it didn't matter as he is perfectly comfortable in the wilderness and wild. Jesus is skilled now in the ways of living off the land and finding shelter. His mind is at ease as he once again marvels at the Father's handiwork. He strides across the landscape.

Jesus seeks the Father's will with every step he makes. It is unusual for a person to be travelling in the wilderness without a companion. So Jesus fully understands the concern of the family he comes upon one afternoon, nearing evening. He approaches their campsite cautiously and, at once, notices the man standing guard at the same time the man sees Jesus.

Stopping his walk, Jesus waves as innocently as he can. He waits for acknowledgement from the man before he proceeds. The man takes his eyes off Jesus and calls over his shoulder. Jesus cannot quite hear the words he speaks, but a lad of about ten or eleven years runs up to the man, and they speak. The boy soon is on a trot toward Jesus.

He approaches Jesus and asks, "My father wants to know who you are and what you want?"

Jesus smiles and calmly responds, "My name is Jesus, and I am a fellow traveler. I am alone. Would you ask your father if I may come to your camp?"

The boy turns and heads back to his father. In a moment, the man waves at Jesus to enter. Jesus strides calmly into their camp. Jesus offers his hand to the man as he approaches, and the man simply waves Jesus forward toward the fire. Jesus nods his acceptance and enters the family circle. As soon as Jesus passes him by, the man discerns a peace and strength about Jesus that instantly calms his being.

"Thank you for accepting me in your circle," Jesus begins. "My name is Jesus, and I am a fellow traveler heading toward my home of Nazareth. I travel alone." As Jesus looks around the gathering, he observes the man, his wife, the boy, and a young girl perhaps twelve or thirteen years of age. There is a strange anguished look on the face of the girl and a tortured manner about her.

She edges up to her mother. Jesus waits for the father of the group to enter the circle around the fire, and when he sits down, Jesus follows suit. The man begins speaking as he motions around the fire, "My name is Caleb. This is my wife Ruth, my daughter Marai, and you've already met my son Simon. We too are on the way to Nazareth to find a physician for our daughter Marai. We are from

111

Cyrene and have already traveled many miles and touched many cities trying to find someone that can heal our daughter. We have been countless months on the road and have suffered untold trials and hardships in our journey. We would welcome your attendance with us to Nazareth as our guide."

While Jesus is taken with compassion for this family, he does not feel as if the Father has ordained he travel with them. But he also feels called to intercede on the behalf of Marai. Jesus understands fully this is no chance meeting in the wilderness, yet he wonders where to begin.

He pauses to gather his thoughts and silently seeks guidance. "Caleb, how do you suppose that YHWH has caused our paths to intersect in the wilderness? The Lord has seen fit to bring us together now in this place. He has given me insight into the cause of Marai's torment and your concern. You must trust me."

Jesus voice and manner has soothed the concerns of Caleb, Ruth, and Simon but has noticeably caused agitation in Marai. She leaves the shelter of her mother's side and straightway approaches Jesus as her face begins to contort. Marai quickly crosses to within a few feet of the seated Jesus and whirls to face her father and curses in a raspy, guttural scowl. "Why have you invited this prophet into our camp! He is powerless against us!" She curses again.

Caleb is stunned to see the misshapen face and the crassness coming from his daughter. He is speechless! He starts to rise to grab his daughter, and she points at him and screams, "Sit down!"

He is powerless to move. Jesus too is taken by the boldness and evil that has manifested in this young girl. Yet he somehow knows this foe and rises to confront this foul creature. The girl no longer physically resembles the daughter. She has been racked by malevolence, and wickedness oozes from her presence. The flames of the campfire exaggerate the malformed facial features and fiery eyes of the fiend now standing before them. The family cannot believe what has overtaken their daughter!

They cower in fear and pray for deliverance. Jesus stands and places his hand upon the shoulder of this girl as she faces her father. The instant of his touch, she screams in excruciating pain! She whirls to face her tormentor, teeth barred! And Jesus commands, "Peace. Be still! You have no power over this child any longer. Leave her now!"

The words have no sooner left his lips when the little girl returns and slumps in a pile to the ground. Ruth rushes to her child's side and covers her with her own body. Caleb jumps to his feet and falls upon them, both weeping with joy. Jesus has recovered and is gazing heavenward with his hands lifted toward the evening stars, whispering to the Father.

Simon stands to his feet and approaches Jesus, unafraid. Simon reaches out to grasp Jesus's shirt and tugs to get his attention. Jesus responds by placing both his hands on Simon's shoulders, to look full in his face. He smiles as he sees the light in the young boy's eyes and drops to his knees, pulling Simon to himself.

Jesus cherishes the embrace. The torment of the frightening moment is over so fast that Caleb, Ruth, and Marai are not quite sure what has happened. They turn and see Simon with his head on Jesus's shoulder and immediately understand what this stranger has done for them. Marai breaks from her parents and runs into the embrace of Jesus, joining Simon.

Jesus kisses her forehead and releases them, standing to look at the amazed parents. "You must see to it that no one knows what I have done here tonight. All praise is to be given to YHWH, for my time has not yet come. I am but a wanderer doing the will of my Father. There will come a day when you will hear of me and miracles and wonders. Seek me then when I can be found, but until that time, tell no man what I have done. I will stay the night with you as you have welcomed me to your fire. On the morrow, I will leave you and take my own path to Nazareth. You will arrive safely and be welcomed there."

Jesus shares a meal with them and soon unrolls his bed to sleep near the fire. The family gathers together to do the same on the other side of the fire. As Jesus settles, he peers across the faltering flames and noticed the eyes of Simon fixated upon him unmoving and unblinking. Jesus smiles and closes his own eyes. The distinct sense of being watched abides with him until he is overtaken with welcome sleep.

The cool night bodes well for a sound sleep, and Jesus wakes early to pack his few things and be off. He tries to be as quiet as possible and not disturb the family and succeeds. Jesus shoulders his pack, and as he strides into the new morning, he pauses to glance back at the resting family.

He is not surprised to see Simon peek out from beneath the covering and wave a good-bye. Jesus's heart is warmed and knows they will cross paths again. Caleb's family makes good time in reaching Nazareth, and it isn't long before they tell of their meeting with a young man named Jesus in the wilderness. They tell anyone who will listen of the miraculous healing of their daughter by this man Jesus's hand. This account soon reaches the ears of Mary, and she is not astounded by it one bit. She longs once again for his imminent return.

Jesus's path to Nazareth is filled with other encounters with travelers and families headed south and west. Each one presents a unique opportunity for Jesus to interact and become aware of people's needs on a personal basis. He finds his stride in intermingling with these individuals and leaving them with a glimpse of the glory yet to be revealed in his ministry.

Along the way, Jesus heals a blind man, cures a woman of leprosy, and uses a lame boy's crutch to fuel a camp fire as he is lame no more. In each case, his power and confidence grows as does his glory in the Father. He leaves each miracle with the admonition to not speak of this happening to anyone along the way.

But of course, none can keep their tongue when it comes to miracles! Jesus's fame begins to spread far and wide. He leaves each with hope and a promise of one day soon seeing the Savior, the Messiah!

Jesus's trek back toward Nazareth lasts a couple of months and includes many more miracles. He soon finds his dusty sandals touching the village border. It has been over four years since Jesus packed his roll and headed to parts unknown. He knows of at least one person who will be glad to see his return.

Ashod's Way

One day, Cris and Daani are sitting in an open-air inn and enjoying doing nothing at all, sipping on new wine. As they talk, the life of Ashod whirls about them at breakneck speed, and they hardly notice. What has caught their attention is the conversation of a group a table away. They are discussing that they had just travelled through Nazareth and the surrounding area and had heard some amazing stories and incidents concerning a man in the wilderness and healing and miracles being performed.

Anytime they heard anything about Nazareth or Bethlehem, they listened closely. This was no exception. It seems more than a few travelers in the wilderness had encountered a lone man who would make friends and perform some kind of miracle or healing before he would melt into the wild again. Now this really had Cris and Daani's full attention, and they leaned closer to listen in. Many of these reports had come pouring in it seems, and this man's name was being spoken of as a rising Hebrew prophet.

Then someone said it! The man's name was Jesus! As they heard this name spoken, both Daani and Cris looked wide-eyed at each other! They couldn't stand it any longer and immediately injected themselves into the conversation.

Standing and grabbing their chairs, they swung them around to face the group, and Daani interrupts by saying, "Do you know what this Jesus guy looks like? or where he said he was from? We grew up with a guy named Jesus many years ago and haven't heard from him in a while."

Cris also chimes in, "Yeah, can you tell us some of the things he's done again? We'd really like to know!"

As the group shares what they have heard about this Jesus, Cris and Daani can hardly believe their ears. But what they are hearing comes as no real surprise; they always had a feeling. They leave the inn that morning, pretty sure this was their Jesus, their old friend.

"Can you believe it?" Cris starts. "Sounds like Jesus has been out in the wilderness finding himself."

"I don't know about all those miracles and stuff, though. Sounds to me like a bunch of mumbo jumbo or magic or something. I mean come on, this is the guy we grew up with and did all those crazy things with! Now he's out healing people and telling people all kinds of things about God stuff. Kind of hard to believe."

Daani offers, "I always had a feeling about him, though. You know like he was special or something like he would do something superior with his life. But you know, you are probably right. How could he heal someone? Or make a cripple walk again? Man, I just don't know!"

Cris says, "Hey, enough of this magic stuff. We've got the real world going on here. We have to meet with Sheba this morning before we get started on our rounds today. Now that's something I can believe in!"

He punches Daani in the arm and picks up the pace toward the temple.

Cris and Daani's rise to the top of the underworld in Ashod can be attributed to one word—*devotion*. They are devoted to Sheba. They are devoted to the temple of Dagon. And they certainly are devoted to the fame and benefits associated with the lifestyle. They seem to lead protected lives when it comes to doing the will of this woman guide of theirs. This duo never wants for a thing. They have nice clothes, a nice place to stay, plenty of money for the things they need and want and all the power associated with the most influential woman in Ashod.

All these things come at a price Cris and Daani could not see or choose not to see. They are blind to the fact they've lost their freedom to think and act on their own. They have lost their compassion for others that where in the same situation as they were not too long before. They owe their allegiance to Sheba and the gods of the Philistines.

They have sold out to their godless nature. They have forsaken the God of their fathers. The God, YHWH, of Abraham, Isaac, and Jacob of whom they had learned and studied as Hebrew children. He is a forgotten space in their mind, filled now with the pleasures of the moment. These same pleasures burn a person out from the inside.

And for the moment, Cris and Daani did not have any problem with that. Sheba greets them at her booth outside the temple wall just like she always does, "And how are my right and left hand this fine day? I am so glad to see you both. I have some important business for you to attend to, but first, today is your special day!"

Cris and Daani know what is coming. Sheba waves her hand over her head and, with grand display, declares, "All the pleasures of the temple await you should you so desire." She smirks devilishly.

Already guessing their wishes, Sheba walks to the back of the booth to pull aside the back wall curtain. Cris and Daani duck behind the curtain. They will not be seen again for a couple of hours or more.

Sheba knows her job well and fully understands the power she wields over these young men. With the benefits these two have come to expect, Sheba is oh so aware they will do anything she asks as soon as she asks it. Inside the temple's larger chamber, Cris and Daani are treated like kings. Their every need and desire is satisfied by a host of willing temple servants.

Special foods, fruits, and drinks are provided as well as a private bathing area, lounge area, and, of course, private chambers. This is a very special affair for them and doesn't happen in any regular time frame. Sheba only appropriates this benefit as she sees fit. Of course, it is all in her plan to control her "help" and keep them eager and hungry.

It seems to have worked wonderfully so far. When Daani and Cris emerge from the temple chamber, Sheba is there to greet them and make sure they are satisfied with their interlude. They were. Sheba sits them down in the booth and closes the outside curtain, signaling passersby she is no longer open for business. Once closed, she glides effortlessly around the booth in the dim light, getting lamps and candles lit for their meeting.

The boys cannot take their eyes off her and watch her every move.

She soon settles in and tells them of their next duty. "Do either of you know a man named Alli?"

"No, well, that is probably just as well."

"Anyway, Alli is a regular at the temple and participates in everything it has to offer on a steady basis. Well, Alli has grown accustomed to all the benefits of the temple and has seen fit to acquire a huge debt that he is now unable to pay. I cannot have this kind of insolence occurring as others will hear of it and think they too can get away without paying. Payment *must* be made! And pay he will!"

Sheba stands and begins to pace back and forth. "So that he and everyone learns a valuable lesson, his payment must be worth more than what he owes! Much more!"

Cris and Daani have very rarely seen Sheba this animated and are giving her their full attention! "I have heard Alli has two very beautiful daughters that have not reached the proper age to be promised yet. Now listen closely you, two! I require *both* of the girls as payment. They are to be servants for the god Dagon in the temple. You, Cris and Daani, will see to Alli's compliance with my payment demands and the girl's safe delivery to the temple priestess."

This is by far the most demanding and difficult task Sheba has given them to complete. This request is a far cry from payment collection or picking up supplies or strong arming someone that doesn't follow proper temple etiquette.

Daani asks meekly, "Are we to figure that Alli does not know your payment demands then?"

Sheba shoots right back, "That is right. He is unaware of the price his indiscretions have cost him. I trust you don't have a problem with this?"

"No, no, of course not, Sheba," Cris interjects. "We are happy to do as you wish anytime."

Their meeting goes on for a couple of more moments as Sheba relates where Alli lives. Then all of a sudden, she is finished with them. Sheba opens up the booth, douses the lights, and greets the afternoon crowd, leaving Cris and Daani to find their own way out.

"Man, how are we gonna manage this one, Cris?" Daani opines as they leave the booth.

"This is big, and Sheba is really worked up about it!"

Cris says, "Yeah, don't worry. We won't let her down."

"I've got a plan."

Daani perks up at Cris's notion of a plan and says sarcastically, "Really? Does that plan include telling Alli or not telling Alli we are taking his daughters to be servants in the temple? I'm just wondering."

Cris retorts, "I won't know for sure until we find out a bit more about our man Alli. You know, is there anything we can hold over his head or just how deep is he really into the goings on of the temple."

"I'm thinking if he's hooked bad enough and wants to continue his illicit shenanigans we've got him. Heck, he'll probably give the girls away himself."

Daani interrupts, "Yeah, well, what if he's a family man and won't part with the girls?"

Cris looks Daani squarely in the face and, as seriously as he can snarls, "That, friend, would be a serious mistake on his part."

A shiver ran up Daani's spine at the thought of what that might entail. "I'm going into the temple to talk with the priest and priestess about our man Alli," Cris says as he heads to the front entrance. "You can stay here. I won't be long."

Daani watches his closest friend in the world walk around the corner and out of view. He can't help but notice the resolve in Cris's stride and the broad shoulders and muscled legs of his cohort and confidante. *Funny,* Daani thinks, *he still keeps his dark hair trimmed liked when we were kids. But, man, is he a handful now. No way I'd ever want to cross him.*

Daani himself has taken on the muscled tone of the streets. Still thin compared to Cris, his shoulders and legs are like twisted rope, long and lean. He wears his shiny, wavy chestnut hair hanging loosely to his shoulders. On occasion, he will tie it gathered back. People say he is quite handsome, but he doesn't see it.

He shrugs his shoulders to himself as he sits and ponders. He does, however, have an uneasy feeling about how their lives have taken this wicked twist, especially after hearing about Jesus in the wilderness and all. Now, those childhood memories are what he would rather think on!

Man, that seems like so long ago, and so many paths and roads and twists and turns. Funny how we have ended up here in Ashod with everything we could want and Jesus has ended up. with seemingly no place to call his own.

Daani sure thought it would be the other way around.

Nazareth Once Again

Jesus stands at Nazareth's threshold. He has a fleeting intuition to turn around and head back into the wild. His mind's eye flashes an image of Mary, and once again, he yearns for her touch and the sound of her voice. He surges ahead.

As Jesus crosses the village, he takes in all the things that are the same yet sees many changes. The biggest change is yet to come. He rounds the last corner before seeing the porch. On the porch sits a woman, head covered and looking down, intent on the work in her lap. Jesus sees the familiar form and does not call out, choosing instead to walk directly to her side. As Jesus approaches, Mary she works diligently and does not notice the man standing at her side until the sun is blocked by his presence. Mary instinctively looks up and cannot quite make out the face of this man as she looks into the sun.

Jesus sees her squint and softly calls her name, "Mary." Instantly, Mary recognizes the voice of her son and leaps to her feet, facing Jesus. Throwing her arms open wide, Jesus drops into her embrace, willingly, a young boy once again in his mind. He lingers on her neck, and the smell of her hair and feel of her skin reinforce his boyhood memories. He relishes this moment of embrace.

And then all too soon, Mary exclaims, "Let me get a look at you!" She pushes Jesus back to look in his face. Right away, she feels his well-defined shoulders and sees the taunt facial features and long hair of a sojourner. She immediately understands that Jesus has changed.

"Son!" Mary cries, "My son! You have returned from your journey of discovery! What stories you must have, and what things you have seen! It has been so long since you have gone. Oh, I have missed you so! Tell me, where you have been and what you have seen?" Mary sits once again and motions for Jesus to sit beside her.

As Jesus sits, he calmly asks, "And how is my father Joseph? I have thought of you both often in my journeys."

With that, Mary hangs her head and begins to weep. Jesus immediately knows and touches Mary's shoulder. Mary looks up and begins, "Joseph became sick about two years after you left, and he never recovered. We did everything we could for him, but he never regained his strength and passed early one morning that fall. I do miss him so. He was a good man and a good father to you. Joseph had so hoped you would return before his passing, but it was not meant to be. He understood you were doing something important and something that must be done."

Mary continues, "He asked me to give to you these written words when you returned. He said you would know what they meant."

Mary reaches inside her outer garment and removes a small leather pouch that she had hanging around her neck. She hands it to Jesus, stands, and says, "I will be inside when you finish."

Jesus takes the pouch in both hands and closes his eyes and slumps into the chair. Upon opening the pouch, Jesus notices a rolled parchment, similar to the ones containing scripture that would be tied into his hair and hung from his clothing as a child. He unties and unrolls the letter.

He smiles and straightens when he recognizes the familiar handwriting of Joseph. Joseph wrote these words:

> Jesus do not weep for me as I now abide
> with the Father, the same Father that sent you
> to be ours. How or why I was chosen to be
> your earthly father, I do not know. But I know
> this: you were my son. I cherished every word
> and every thought and every moment we had

together. The labor we shared and the fruits of
our handiwork testify to the fact you are mine.
All of heaven adores you as will all of earth. I love
you and await your return.

The writing ends too abruptly for Jesus. Oh, how he longs for
more letters, more words, more sentences. But there are no more.
Such as it is here on this earth, he thinks. The words end, and the
memories are all you have left. And all too soon, even the memories
become dim.

Jesus clings to the last sentence, "I love you and await your
return." Now there is hope! Jesus smiles at that thought. Jesus slowly
rises from the seat and rolls the parchment to place it in the pouch
where it had resided for years awaiting his eyes. He hangs it around
his neck and tucks it under his shirt. It soon takes on the same
warmth as his own body.

Jesus gathers himself and heads into the house. He calls, "Mary,
mother, I am here."

Mary answers from the kitchen, "In here, Jesus, in here."

Jesus walks in to the room and finds Mary seated at the table.
Before her sit bread and wine in earthenware. Jesus sits looking at
Mary without a word. The solitude seems to last forever and then
Jesus speaks, "I wish that I had known my father was ill. I could have
been here for you."

"No, Jesus, all is well here. The dead will care for themselves.
You must attend to the living."

Jesus finds wisdom and insight in these words. As they break
bread and sip wine, Mary fills Jesus in on the goings on in Nazareth
and such. Jesus takes it all in and then inquires, "What have you
heard of Bethlehem since we left and what about my old friends
Daani and Cris? Any word on what they are doing?"

Mary casts a long glance at Jesus before answering, "Well, it
seems that Cris and Daani got into some sort of trouble. It involved
beating up a man to protect a little girl. There was a hearing, a trial.
It didn't go well for them I'm told. They ended up getting lashed
and sentenced to jail time. Not long after their release, they headed

off to Philistine country. The last I heard they were in Ashod, you know, where the temple of Dagon is. Nothing good ever comes from Ashod." She ends and wags her head in a "so sad" motion.

The breath is snatched from his core as Jesus sits in disbelief at what has transpired with his old allies, his childhood friends. Words cannot describe the anguish in his heart over the pain they must have experienced. Mary senses Jesus's distress and offers, "What they have experienced cannot be changed. My only hope for them is in the teachings of the scriptures they learned as children that they remember and take heed."

She continues, "There is more, Jesus. It is being said they are intimately involved with the temple and its goings on. They are some kind of bodyguards or street thugs for the god Dagon. Only YHWH knows what they are really involved in."

Jesus's mind is whirling. "I should go and find them and bring them back. Maybe I could change their minds or show them or something!"

Mary feels the turmoil and can only offer, "They are young men, just as you are now. They have made choices to be in the place and situation they are in. Do you really think you can change their minds? You must think long and hard and seek the Father's wisdom before you seek them, if you seek them out in Ashod."

Jesus knows his mother is right. This would not be something he should consider lightly and without divine guidance. He decides to pray over this decision. Although Jesus's mind is spinning with all he has heard from Mary, he needs to share with her what has transpired in his life these past four years. He notices the shadows lengthening as the fading daylight gives way to night and senses this will be a long time of sharing ahead. He knows of no one he would rather be talking to than his mother.

Jesus begins where he left Nazareth. He ends with his return to Nazareth. Mary is amazed with all that fills up the middle—the travel by foot over miles and miles of desert and mountains, the hunting and fending for himself and God's provision, the prophet Eli alive and living in the wild and his return to heaven, the blindness and finding his way, the presence of the Almighty and hearing and feeling Him speak, the lion as protector, the lessons of this life and its death, the revelation of his purpose and divine guidance, the prayer, the fasting, the healings, and His godhead revealed.

It has all been spoken now, and Mary has heard every word that Jesus has offered. It is now Mary's turn to have her mind spinning. She now knows that the fullness of the godhead is present in her son Jesus. She knows now that his path has been established and ordained. She knows also that this will not be an easy or desirable path. She does not fully understand yet the pain and suffering he must endure. For if she could see that, Mary would surely tell Jesus to run away and never return!

The Price of Captivity

Daani sits and waits for Cris's return not really aware of the hustle and bustle around him. He doesn't mind waiting because he knows as soon as Cris comes back, they will be off. To do what exactly, he is not sure. But he is certain of one thing. It is not going to end well for someone.

He knows they owe everything they have to Sheba and her provision for them. In return, they have offered her unfailing loyalty and devotion. But most of all, they have never questioned one of her assignments. This latest mission will test their loyalty to its ends and stretch their devotion to its breaking. That is in Daani's mind anyway.

Now Cris, on the other hand, Daani muses, *would certainly give his own life for Sheba if it was ever required. Man, he's still got it bad.* Daani's thoughts are broken by the familiar whistle of his partner's return. Daani looks up but still cannot see Cris, so he stands and looks into the crowd in the street. Finally, Cris pops into view and waves for Daani to join him as he heads in the opposite direction. Daani breaks into a trot to gain Cris's side.

Cris does not slow his pace one bit and strides with determination toward the north gate of Ashod. Daani finally, out of desperation, reaches out and grabs Cris's arm to slow him down and says, "Hey, Cris! Ease up a bit there. Come on, man! Are you going to tell me what happened and what you found out, and where are going?"

Cris shakes Daani's hand from his arm, whirls around, and faces him full on. The scowl on Cris's face says it all, and Daani inches back just a little. Daani couldn't tell whether Cris was ready to cry or fight or both! He knew one thing, though. Cris needed to settle down and fill him in, or this is going to be even more difficult for both of them.

As chance would have it, they stopped away from the crowd, and there was a tree nearby they could sit beneath and take a deep breath. It was Daani who lead Cris this time to the shade and out of the foot traffic. As they sit down, Daani can see the shaking hands and the flushed face of his best friend. He is worried.

"I went in to the temple to find out more about this guy Alli and his family and where he lives," Cris begins. "I was talking to the temple people and getting some good information, stuff I thought we could use when out of nowhere, Sheba is breathing down my neck and becomes irate that I would be talking about this to anyone but her! I mean, she was not nice! She really made me look bad in front of a lot of people in there." A visible shiver passes over Cris as he thinks back on the encounter. "And I don't like looking bad! And while she is causing this scene, people are starting to notice, and soon, everyone is turned and listening to her scream at me! And that is not the worst of it!

"Seems our man Alli was in one of the private rooms, comes out, and figures out we're talking about him and goes running out of the temple! Now you got the picture? This deed just got a whole lot more complicated all because of that...that...woman!"

"Well, that doesn't sound all that bad to me," quips Daani. "Sheba might have done us a big favor!"

Cris roars back, "What, are you crazy? Alli knows we are on to him now, and he'll take the girls and run!"

"Take it easy, Cris, okay? I have an idea," Daani starts. "Just think about this for a second now. If we can get to his place and wait for him to run with the girls, are you following me here? We got him in the open and away from his home and rest of the family. Not bad huh?" And Daani smiles.

Cris finally relaxes a bit and nods affirmatively at Daani. "Yeah, that's not bad buddy, not bad at all. We can work out more of the details as we head toward Alli's place. And by the way," Cris continues, "Alli is into the temple big time. He owes a ton of money with no way to pay it back, and it doesn't seem like he has any desire to break any of his bad habits. He's hooked."

As they clear the hubbub of the north gate of the city, they almost get the feeling of freedom again. Almost. Cris offers, "It feels good to be out of the city. You know, we don't get out much anymore, and I miss the fresh air and openness. We should do this more often."

"Yeah," Daani says. "We are really tied to the city and the temple, and we owe Sheba our souls! It doesn't feel like we can do anything on our own. We always have someone telling us what to do."

"You do know that that is our job, right? We do other people's bidding," Cris answers, kind of annoyed. "I don't hear you complaining about the fringe benefits and a great place to stay and plenty of money in our pockets. Besides, where would we be if we hadn't come to Ashod?"

Cris is on a roll now and switches into his best mode of sarcasm. "Better yet, we'd be out wandering in the desert like our old friend Jesus, all delusional about healing people and changing people and being God's son, and I really like this one, being the promised Messiah! Wow, what a fool!"

Cris is heading into verbal territory that Daani is not comfortable with one bit. But he bites his lip and says nothing. If he doesn't take the bait, Daani knows Cris will drop it, and this is not the time or the place to get in an argument with Cris. Besides, they need to figure out exactly what they are going to do when they find Alli.

Daani breaks the strain of the conversation by asking, "So where are we going, and how far is Alli's place out of town?"

"Well," Cris answers, "supposedly, he lives in a small gathering of family members about three miles north of Ashod. The priest said we couldn't miss it because it is right at the base of the only big hill near the seashore, and it's before we cross the river. He said there weren't any other people living around them. He thought there would be three tents kind of hooked together with a wooden barricade surrounding them. It should be pretty easy to find."

"Which brings me to my next big question," Daani says. "What are we going to do when we find him?"

"Right now, we only have your plan in play, you know, wait for him to run with the girls and follow and snatch them when we get a chance." Cris eyes Daani as he finishes and continues, "You are okay with that, right?"

"Yeah, sure I'm okay with it. It's just that saying it is a whole lot easier than actually doing it!" Daani retorts.

"Well, you are probably right about that," says Cris. We should be coming up to his place real quick now. Let's start being more careful and quiet until we get a lay of the land."

They have been off the regular road that headed for Jabneel for about the last mile and are walking along a fairly good path now. Soon, they should see the settlement of Alli and his family. It is nearing sundown, and light is beginning to fade, so their wish is for contact before dark.

Daani whispers, "Do you think he'll try and take the girls out tonight yet, Cris?"

"The way I figure it, he had about an hour head start on us if he really moved once he left the temple. I would think he has some major explaining to do to his wife if he's going to move the girls tonight. Our timing should be just right, if tonight is the night," Cris ends abruptly as they round a slight bend in the path and come into view of three structures with a fence surrounding them all nestled at the base of a big hill.

Throwing up his hand to signal stop, Cris and Daani step off the path and into the rocks and bushes. They have a clear view of the buildings from about fifty yards away and notice they sit in the open with only a few palm trees behind them. Cris notes a few gulls flying in the air and figures from the top of the hill behind the house, you would have a clear view of the Great Sea to the west, about a mile away.

"If it happens tonight, we shouldn't have too long of a wait," Cris whispers. "Let's make ourselves comfortable and see if anything happens before it gets real dark."

They wait, and darkness soon engulfs them. The temperature begins to cool as the prevailing winds from the west push cooler moist air inland. Just when they had figured nothing would happen this night, noise and shouting and torch lights and lamps erupt from the compound! It comes from the middle dwelling.

There is a woman screaming and cursing, and they can hear the sounds of children crying too. A man's gruff voice can be heard above all the ruckus, yelling and screaming in response. They see one torch move to the east toward another building and hear more cursing as the sounds of a cart and animal being readied ring in the night. The torch returns to the center of the enclosure along with the squeaky wheels of a cart on the move.

The screams and cries turn into wails. What a horrific sound! It pierces the darkness and is carried off to the east by the wind bouncing between the hills. Cris and Daani are on full alert now! The hair on the back of their necks is standing straight, and their eyes are open wide, straining for any advantage over the darkness.

All they can see is what the torches reveal in their ten-foot area of influence. The chaos has not subsided. They glimpse the man grabbing at a small girl and flinging her into the cart. The man turns and is set upon by the woman, fists flailing. He pushes the woman to the ground and grabs another kicking and screaming girl and flings her into the cart, landing atop the other. The man hastily throws a blanket over the sobbing, screaming forms.

Daani cannot believe the scene before his eyes. The darkness lends to the surreal nature of this battle of wills before him as do the shadows of flickering lamplights. He shakes his head in disbelief as he witnesses an entire family torn apart. Lives will be forever altered as a result of the sum of the actions taken tonight, and the grief isn't over yet, he knows.

Daani trembles at the thought of the anguish he and Cris will bring upon this family also. This deed is far from over; in fact, it is just beginning! The man Alli finally breaks free from the skirmish he has created and feverishly whips the small donkey. The cart and its precious contents slowly rumble off into the night.

The distraught woman emerges from the compound, crawling on her hands and knees, accompanied by a mournful moan. She soon is enveloped in darkness. The moaning ends as does all sounds of the night, save for the squeaking sound of the cart wheels as they reach further into the darkness. The woman lays exhausted, heart pierced, and spent. She can weep no more.

Cris and Daani watch the single lamplight from the cart get smaller and smaller until all that remains is a faint glimmer in the distance. Sure that all the others are back in the dwellings, they break from the hide now covered by the moonless dark. They stride off replete in the old confidence that comes with their many years of backing each other without fail.

However, this confrontation will be unlike any they have ever experienced. Soon, they notice every stride they take makes the cart light loom larger and larger. Until once again, they make out the form of the man leading the donkey and the cart. It's cargo covered by a blanket. No sound apart from the squeaky wheel is heard unless you count their wildly beating hearts.

Their plan is simple. They need the donkey and cart to deliver the girls to the temple. They must separate Alli from the girls and cart. They will try diplomacy first. Cris will circle out and get ahead of the ensemble and pick a clear spot. Cris will confront Alli and make sure he understands, in no uncertain terms, that payment is now due. And that his debt will be paid in full when both girls enter the temple as servants. If Alli doesn't understand the terms of this transaction, then there will be more explaining on Cris's part, which probably means an escalation in the coarseness of the rhetoric. Daani is to stay back, out of the light's influence, and when he hears the creaking stop, he will move in and stay behind the cart, hidden.

The night abruptly turns silent. Daani makes his move, and Cris is suddenly in Alli's way. Then the unthinkable happens! Alli reaches behind his back and draws out a short curved sword. The blade gleams as it arcs in the pale light. He swings it in front of and across his body, inserting the blade into the bright-blue sash tied about his waist. The blade rests now at his right side. This action by Alli was not directed at Cris but to show his readiness.

Daani tenses as Cris calmly walks into the circle of light, exposing himself fully, hands raised to show he has no weapon. Cris, now with his hands fully extended in front, begins, "Whoa there, Alli, I mean no harm to you or the girls." He stops speaking and stops his approach.

After taking a few seconds to size up the situation and noticing Daani in the shadows behind, Cris continues, "I am simply here to collect payment for your overdue debt at the temple. You know what is required. The price that Sheba requires is your two daughters delivered to the temple immediately! You will give them to me now, and I will be on my way."

Daani notices that Cris has kept the conversation to draw attention to himself alone. *Smart,* he thinks. *Alli doesn't even know I'm here.*

Alli finally speaks, and it is with trembling and fear in his voice, "I have become addicted to all the pleasures and everything the temple has to offer. I owe my soul to the god Dagon, but my daughters have done nothing to deserve the fate that awaits them in your hands! I beg of you, let me take them far away from here! Far from the reach of Dagon!"

At this notion, Cris begins to laugh a sinister laugh. "You think you can run from Dagon and Sheba? It is your debt to pay! Sheba has set the payment. I am simply here to collect. Now!"

Alli trembles. Confronted and accused, a defeated man. Head down and shoulders slumped forward, he perceives his enemy standing before him, when in his heart he knows his true enemy lies inside—himself. He recognizes his own destiny has been sealed when he sold his soul to the temple. He can no longer bear thinking of his daughters as slaves to the temple.

In a blink of the eye, the unimaginable is set in motion. Cris and Daani are caught off guard and are mesmerized by the swiftness of the blade. A dark presence, a pall, flashes across the face of Alli. He whirls away from Cris and raises the sword in one deft motion, a two-handed death grip upon its handle. Alli advances on the whimpering shapes huddled beneath the blankets with sword held high above his head.

A tormented shriek crosses his lips, almost a scream! The blade's deadly arc heads down, parting the cool night air. It's travel is intercepted by a pale flash of cinnamon hair that comes from the shadows to the rear of the cart. The trajectory of the blade is momentarily deflected as it slices through locks of hair and sets hard into a shoulder blade.

Daani's leap has taken the brunt of the swing meant as a death blow for the girls. The momentum of the leap has delivered Daani beneath the arms of Alli and squarely into his chest. Alli is knocked from his feet, and Daani lands on top, pinning him to the ground.

Cris rushes forward to aid his partner and sees the sword standing on edge in Daani's back. He gasps at the sight. Cris's shock turns instantly into rage, and he falls upon the prostrate Alli and lands one well-placed blow to the head, sending him into personal darkness.

Daani feels the limp body beneath him and tries to push himself up and off. The pain tears through his shoulder with the swiftness of an arrow in flight. He winces out loud, and then the pain overcomes his senses.

Daani loses consciousness and covers the body beneath with his.

Blood begins to stain the outer garment as its circle quickly enlarges before Cris's eyes. Panic begins to set in as Cris surveys the situation. He also is aware of a stirring beneath the blanket in the bed of the cart, but Daani needs him more right now.

As gently as possible, Cris grabs Daani's shoulders and lifts, dragging him from atop the still form of Alli. "Hey, buddy! Daani! Man, are you okay?" He worries aloud.

There is no answer. Cris grabs the lamp from the cart and kneels beside Daani to get a better look. Daani lays face down. The blade of the sword is standing, backbone up. *If there wasn't so much blood, it would almost look fake,* Cris thinks.

Cris hears a faint moan from Daani and simultaneously hears soft cries from the back of the cart. His head and mind are whirling. Cris runs back to the cart and yells at the hidden shapes, "You'll be okay as long as you stay beneath the blanket. Do not move!"

Once again, he turns his attention to Daani who has regained a hands-and-knees posture. Cris drops to his knees beside his friend and lays his left hand on Daani's back to steady his platform.

"Don't move, Daani. I don't know how bad the injury to your back is yet. I really have to get a look!" Cris begins to peel back

Daani's shirt and reveals the blade stuck in the top of the shoulder bone. It looks to be in about a half an inch deep and not too solidly stuck, but the cut is about three inches long and still bleeding.

Cris tells Daani, "I've got to try and get the sword out of your shoulder to wrap your wound. This might hurt a bit!"

Daani grunts a response. The handle of the sword sits near Daani's head. Cris rests his left hand on Daani's head, grabs the handle with his right hand, and pulls up with one motion. The blade slides from its wedge surprisingly easy.

"It's out! I got it, Daani!" Cris cries with triumph.

Daani is not so enthusiastic about the whole ordeal and remains on hands and knees, head down, and body swaying to an uneven rhythm. Cris searches frantically for something to rip apart for a bandage and finds nothing. He then rushes to the back of the cart and snatches the blanket, tearing it from its purpose. The revelation of the girls causes Cris to jump in surprise as the two begin a loud whining, clutching one another tightly.

Cris stutters in shock, "I...I...'m sorry! I didn't mean to scare you. I need the blanket for my friend. Stay there. I'll be right back for you." But he cannot move, neither can he take his eyes from the girls in the cart now exposed to the lamplight. Cris has never really considered the humanness of this action of theirs. And now they exist right before his eyes—two beautiful little girls frightened to death and crying in the night.

Cris shakes his head violently from side to side, trying to clear his mind and remember the reason they are here, and then Daani moans. His jaded purpose realized once more, Cris turns and trots to Daani to wrap his wound. Tearing the blanket as he moves, he sits Daani down and adjusts the lamplight for best coverage and gently begins winding the pieces around the injured shoulder with quaking hands.

Man, that is a lot of blood, Cris thinks, *but the wound looks clean and not too gaping.* Daani seems to be regaining his composure. "I don't know if you'll need to get sewn up, but we can leave that to Sheba when we get back to Ashod," Cris offers. "The girls look to be okay. They are pretty scared, though. And here, I've got something for you. It is only right that you should have it." Cris hands the sword to Daani as he struggles to his feet. Daani takes it, looks it over, and slides it into his waist sash to the hilt.

He steadies himself by placing his hands on the side of the cart. At this point, Cris picks up the lamp and raises it above the cart, fully revealing both girls in its light. They lay huddled together, eyes wide open, shivering and terrified. Daani is shocked at how very, very young they look.

As they stand in the lamplight, they see motion in front of the donkey and look at each other in forgetful alarm. Alli!

They have completely forgotten about him as he lay unconscious! He is awake now and wastes no time in vanishing into the night on a very unsteady run. Out of instinct, Cris lurches a couple of strides to pursue him, and Daani yells, "Don't, Cris! We don't need him anymore. Let the coward run! He's doing us a big favor!"

Cris relaxes and returns. "Man, you are right again! Besides, we got what we came after."

He finds the remains of the torn blanket and hands it to the girls. "I'm sorry, but this is the best we can do for you right now. We'll be back in Ashod before long."

The darkness is quickly running its course as they slowly make their way back to Ashod. Cris leads the donkey by its bridle, and Daani is steadying himself as best he can. He rests his right hand upon the back of the donkey as it plods along. Neither of them dare peer into the back of the cart.

The girls have been quiet for most of the journey. And if they made any noise, it would be covered by the squeaking of the wheel anyway. Soon, their responsibility for them will end, at least in their own minds. What a pitiful, sorrowful troupe this is. Ashod cannot get here too soon.

Auspicious Return

As soon as the Cris-and-Daani-led procession clears the north gate, people begin to take notice. The murmuring and whispering and pointing precedes the troupe all the way through the streets.

While Cris is certainly no worse for the wear, Daani is walking on wobbly legs and is covered by a blood-soaked shirt. The girls peer frightfully from under the torn blanket as the only cargo in the cart. This certainly is not a triumphant return by anyone's estimation. By the time the motley unit stumbles to the bottom step of the temple, they have gathered quite an assemblage of followers.

Cris calls out to those temple workers in earshot, "Someone get Sheba! Now!"

He turns and eases Daani down on the second step. Daani slumps into his arms, and Cris props him up. "Hey, man, we made it. We are at the temple, and Sheba will be here in a second. We'll get you all fixed up as soon as she gets here! Hang in there, friend!" Cris begins to get anxious and whirls around to see if anyone has summoned Sheba yet.

Sheba stands at the top of the steps back near the arch into the temple. She talks and gestures wildly with two of the temple guards. One of them is the chief. And then she abruptly turns and marches back into the temple.

The guards hustle across the platform and down the thirteen steps to Cris. The chief of guards goes directly to Cris, and the other takes the donkey and cart and heads around the west side of the temple, out of sight. Cris watches the back of the cart disappear and sees two little heads pop up from under the torn blanket, eyes wide with terror.

He wishes he had not seen that. The chief stands next to the duo and says, "You are to come with me to the east wall entrance at Sheba's tent. You will be attended to there."

The guard turns to walk around to the east wall of the temple, and Cris yells, not asking but telling, "Hey there, Chief! A little help with Daani here!" The guard hears the intent in Cris's voice and immediately returns to shoulder Daani's other arm.

The two drag and shuffle Daani around the corner. The gathered witnesses disperse, unfulfilled. And the temple hawkers once again drown out any thoughts or words, save for the hustle in the streets. Cris and Daani enter through the familiar tent-side entry and are soon in the coolness of the inner chamber of the temple. Daani is laid upon a floor mat and soon has two temple maids attending to him. They remove his bloodied shirt and bring a laver of water and a cloth to begin washing his wound and back.

Cris sits alone off to the side, head down, dejected and upset. He doesn't even notice when Sheba glides up to him. He instantly comes out of his funk when she sits down, close to him. Very close to him.

Without saying a word, Sheba puts her arm around Cris and pulls him to her right side. Taking his head in her left hand, she pulls him even closer and rests her chin on the top of his head. Cris is speechless and breathless! And to further muddle his mind, she smells unbelievable!

Sheba coos softly, "My brave, brave Cris. I knew I could count on you and Daani to accomplish my wishes. You have done more than I could have hoped for. The girls are beautiful and are perfect. I will see to Daani also and make sure he is well cared for and perfectly mended. I need you both!" As Sheba caresses Cris's face, she continues, "I don't know what I would do without you!"

Sheba knows that Cris is completely under her spell at this moment. She could ask him to move heaven and earth, and he would attempt it. She sees a perfect chance to control Cris and even further set this one-sided love affair. Sheba offers, "I will have a bath drawn for you." She signals another of the temple women to her side and whispers some orders into her ear. The only thing Cris can make out is the end of the command, and he hears, "And see to it that everything is perfect!"

Cris glances toward Daani and sees the temple doctor has arrived and is preparing to sew up the wound. The women are still in attendance, and Cris is sure they won't be leaving Daani anytime soon. "Do you think Daani will be okay, Sheba?" he asks.

Sheba laughs and winks. "I'm pretty sure that after the doc is done, Daani will have plenty of other things to take his mind off his injury! Your bath should be ready now, and I want to make sure everything is just right for you. Come with me, Cris."

Sheba stands and takes Cris by the hand and leads him to one of the private rooms. She parts the curtain covering the entry and peers inside. From the outside, you can see a dimly lit interior with flickering candlelight casting shadows and shapes on the walls.

A sweet odor wafts from the room—the aroma of flowers. The smell of hot scented oil reaches out from the room and fills Cris's mind and senses. Sheba disappears behind the curtain and is gone for an eternity in Cris's mind. In a second, a hand emerges from behind the curtain to wave Cris inside. There is no hesitation as he swings the curtain aside. The drape flutters and then is closed.

Journey toward Perdition

Jesus spends five or six months with Mary in Nazareth. The bond between mother and son is renewed and strengthened. As only mothers can, Mary senses Jesus once again needing freedom and a change from the safety of this village home. Jesus also has been increasingly concerned about what is happening in Ashod to Cris and Daani. After much prayer and seeking, he feels drawn to the Philistine country. He only needs encouragement from Mary.

One day, they were sitting in the shade talking about everything and nothing when Mary reads Jesus's heart and says, "My son, perhaps you should consider the path into Philistine country and Ashod. We have long heard of the degradation and immorality of men in this region. Perhaps you should see for yourself. And of course, you can look up your old friends Cris and Daani while you are there. I'm sure they would even put you up while you visit."

Jesus answers, "Mother, again you have seen my heart and the Father's desire for me to grow. I will leave on the morrow." Indeed, Mary has had more than an insight into her son's heart. She has had a glimpse of the evil Jesus will witness in Ashod, and it sends a chill to her core. However, she also is aware that Jesus has grown in strength and wisdom and will be more than able to face this challenge, his adversary.

Somehow, she knows his time has not yet come to fulfill his ultimate destiny. The next morning, early before sunrise, Mary has prepared Jesus a few days' supplies and bundled his bedroll. She anticipates his awakening and eventual departure. No longer racked with grief and worry about his travels, she understands completely now. She exudes confidence in the plan YHWH has for her son.

Mary sings softly as she waits for Jesus. The tune imprints on his heart as he readies to leave. Jesus has sweetly kissed the cheek of his mother and now turns to walk from her presence for another sojourn and challenge. His reason now renewed, Jesus heads west and wants to reach Philistine country as soon as possible. He realizes that this decision will mean his path south to Ashod will reside within Philistine land for nearly eighty miles and consume four or five days.

He has always wanted to visit the coastline of the Great Sea. Water, as far as you can see, will be a welcome relief from the dry desert land he recently returned from. His pace is lively as this new adventure beckons. Jesus has time to think as he walks with the sun to his back. His thoughts promptly turn to Cris and Daani, and he calls out to the Almighty, "Father, I do not know what I will find as I traverse this land of the Philistines. I trust You now for Your guidance and direction, wisdom and strength. The gods of men's hearts do not compare to You and Your wisdom, and I pray that everyone I come in contact with will leave knowing You. As I seek my friends, I ask for wisdom to be imparted to them at our meeting. Give me sight into their hearts, I pray. Amen."

Jesus's first day of travel brings him to the rim of the valley called Megiddo. As he surveys the basin that stretches before, he is overtaken with a powerful foreboding. *Strange,* he thinks as he studies the landscape. Jesus can see the scars of battles previously fought in the valley and surrounding hills, but these are not the source of his ominous feelings. He also has the impression he will return to this same valley in the future. A shiver passes through his being and then is gone. It becomes apparent he needs to put some distance between himself and Megiddo.

Jesus figures he has a couple of hours before sunset. That should be plenty of time for him to cross the valley and reach the west rim of Megiddo. He'll try to lay eyes on the Great Sea before nightfall.

The valley and the west wall prove to be a challenge Jesus is not willing to expend all his energy on right now. He settles on a camp just short of the west wall as its shadows surround his fresh fire. A chill quickly engulfs him, so much so that he unrolls his bed and drapes it over his shoulders as he watches the fire's comforting dance. Jesus unpacks the food bag Mary had prepared and undoes the string to reveal fresh bread and dried meat. He smiles at the picture of Mary still new in his mind. He finds himself humming the same song she had been singing when he stirred this morning.

Jesus pulls the scriptures from his pack and settles in to read from the writings of the prophet Isaiah. He begins reading the fortieth chapter. The greatness of the Father is revealed! As he finishes the chapter, he reads aloud, "Those whose hope is YHWH will renew their strength. They will soar on wings like eagles. They will run and not grow weary. They will walk and not be faint."

"Father, my hope is in You!" Jesus concludes as he snuggles down into his bed for the night. He rests with his face to the dying fire. The embers are the last thing he remembers of the day as a smile crosses his lips.

He sits with a start surrounded by darkness, wailing in the night, gnashing of teeth, cries, screams! Had they come from him? Jesus can't tell whether he is awake or dreaming. The darkness sits upon him like a cloak. He shakes from the cold sweat of the revelation. He cannot speak as the freshness of the visions have taken his breath. Vivid foresight of destruction and war—such as this earth has never before seen, a battle to end all battles, blood flowing around headless corpses, and finally, the *light* without shadows that causes the darkness to flee for eternity!

He stands in the darkness and feels around to gather his things to pack his bag. He has stayed long enough in this place. He doesn't care that he will be traveling in the darkness of a moonless night; he must leave. As Jesus looks up to get his bearing from the stars, he sees an intense light resting on the rim of the west wall. It is focused on his face, yet it is not blinding! The stars reverberate the voice that emanates from the light, "Come to the light!" And he obeys.

As Jesus focuses on the light, his footsteps are effortless, barely feeling the earth. If he looks away, he is instantly reconnected with the rocks and sand and unsure footing. It doesn't take long to realize he needs to center his attention completely upon the light! Jesus reaches the position of the light and is overcome by the intensity of the brightness, yet is glorified by its presence.

The voice speaks softly. "My Son, I have given you a glimpse of the coming darkness. You are headed into the manifestation of this same darkness in your travels south. Be aware of your adversary who roams about like a great beast seeking those he may consume. You are approaching a den of this prince of darkness. You must never lose sight of the light that shines in you. You are that light. You are humankind's only hope of redemption. You can redeem only those who accept your Living Word. Never lose heart!"

"You have been sent by the Great I Am!"

Jesus closes his eyes to savor the presence of YHWH and His Words, letting it all sink in. He does not speak. The moment turns into minutes, and the minutes turn to hours. Finally, this marvelous interlude dissolves. Jesus feels the warmth of the new sun on his back. His eyes open, and he turns to witness the dawn of a new day. Ah, the eastern sky!

"Glorious!" he exclaims. The first step of the new day causes Jesus to recall the warning from the Father. "I have heard Your Words and have placed them in my heart. I seek only Your will in my travels. Father, guide me this day! Amen!"

He does not look back at the valley of Megiddo and shudders at the thought of the visions. He raises each sandaled foot and shakes it vigorously in the air, dislodging as much of the dust and sand from the valley as possible. He thinks out loud, "No use carrying that with me for the rest of my journey!" and trudges on to the southwest. Jesus wonders what he will find in Ashod. He wonders just how deep into the culture his friends are immersed. He wonders if anything good will come from this journey.

"I guess that's why I'm headed in that direction!" he says to no one in particular and then laughs at himself. He has finally reached the Plain of Sharon and left the hill and mountainous country behind for the time being. As the ground levels out, Jesus can sense a change in the breeze—sea air! How refreshing and different.

He turns due west, eager to witness and feel the sea for the first time in his life. There before him, the glimmer of the water looks like thousands of crystals, each calling to him. He increases his pace and soon stands on the sandy shore of the Great Sea. Wonder of wonders! Its expanse goes on forever!

He sits and removes his sandals and joyously wades into the surf. The water is so calm his splashing creates rings that hurry away from the shoreline until out of sight. And blue! And clear! And warm! Jesus stoops to gather a handful of the clear water. He instinctively brings it to his lips and sips. Wrong idea! The harshness of the salt and warmth of the shallows makes him gag!

Funny, he thinks, *so inviting, available and abundant but no good for drinking! Another lesson in the making.* Jesus has been consumed with the shoreline and the sea until now. He stops to look north and then south along the beach and can see nothing in either direction. Perfect! He also notices the sand has a clean windswept look to it with no human footprints in sight. He will keep his travel southward along the shore until nightfall.

He sees many strange and wonderful creatures, big and small, in the sand and in the waters. There are little fishes darting to and fro being chased by bigger fishes. Crabs and shells and crabs in shells! Gulls making all sorts of racket as they try to catch food. *Strange*, he thinks, *if they were only more quiet!*

Marvelous! The sea has proven to be all he hoped for and more. The Almighty's handiwork is in full display! The evening is upon Jesus all too soon, and he must choose a camp for the night. He must be nearing the village of Hepher. Some signs of other travelers and civilization are now evident. Jesus heads away from the shoreline a couple of hundred yards and makes a camp near some small trees. He gets a small fire going just as the sun sets over the still, calm sea. *Beautiful! What could be more perfect*, he thinks as he pulls bread and wine from his pack.

Intent on the fire and fading sunlight, Jesus is caught unaware by two men circling from behind, one on each side. Jesus looks up with a start and then smiles. "Hello, friends, what can I do for you?" He remains seated, cross-legged next to the fire.

Jesus can tell in a glance that these two are not to be trusted. And the conversation soon bares that feeling out. "Well, lad," the one on the right begins, "we are just wondering where you are headed and who you are travelling with."

Jesus offers with a steady voice, "My name is Jesus, and I travel from Nazareth on my way to Ashod to look up some old friends and see the city. I travel alone."

"A Nazarene headed to Ashod huh?" The one on the left slurs, "You headed there to have some fun in the temple and spend all your money?" He kind of chuckles at the thought.

Jesus doesn't even respond to that inquiry and says, "You are welcome to sit with me and share what I have for dinner. It is not much, but it should go around." He motions, "Please sit."

The man on the right is instantly agitated and curses. "Enough of this small talk! Give us everything you have now! And we may let you live!" Both men take an offensive posture as they each pull a small-bladed knife from their belts and wave them in the firelight. Jesus sits calmly in the same light. He does not speak or look them in the face. His demeanor is fueling their rage!

"Did you not hear me, son of a Hebrew donkey?" The man takes a step closer to Jesus, and Jesus looks up into the man's wild eyes. He has glimpsed this hatred before.

Jesus raises his hand and says, "You have not come to my camp by accident tonight. Know this. I would gladly give you all that I possess if you would sit with me and talk and then peacefully go your way."

"You idiot!" the man yells. "We'll go our way when you are lying there, gutted and bleeding!" Both men try to move forward, and they are held in place by an unseen hand. They look at each other with astonishment and open their mouths to speak, but they are struck dumb!

The men look at Jesus, bewildered! Jesus has risen next to the fire and begins softly, "You have not listened to reason. Therefore, I surmise you are unreasonable men with malice alone in your hearts." Jesus's tone abruptly changes as he forcefully continues, "You will listen to me now, however! You will turn from this fire and head to the edge of the sea. Once at water's edge, you will turn south and follow the shoreline until you reach the next village about forty miles away. No one will come to your aid in this journey. You will be set upon by others, even unto death. The darkness tonight will remain with you until you pass from this life. You will be blinded from this moment on! Leave this place now!"

The men are released from the hold upon them. They turn and stumble into the abyss of the night. Jesus is shaken visibly by this encounter and harsh lesson he has meted out. He also made a discovery. He recognized the wickedness in these men's hearts and their evil desires before they spoke. He can use this acumen in the future.

Jesus surveys all that is within the light cast by the small fire. He sees provisions and bedroll and something in the sand where the two stood. The knives! They dropped their knives as they stumbled away! Jesus retrieves them from the sand. As he looks at these tools, he thinks of the perversion that has controlled their use. Such simple devices, yet when controlled by evil hearts, they can change lives and futures in an instant.

The bloodstains etched into the metal were caused by the evil in men's hearts. There is no will in the knife. He soon realizes he is exhausted and welcomes the calmness and coolness of the evening. He needs to be refreshed. Sleep will be his ally tonight.

The new day dawns, and as Jesus packs, he comes across the two knives again. Taking them into the brush, he finds a suitable rock pile and digs his way into it. Satisfied they will be buried further by the shifting sands, he tucks the blades back in the hole and restacks the pile.

As he heads south again, he is struck by the fact that this trip has not started out very well. "I guess I shouldn't be surprised," Jesus muses. "It will be a time of lessons and learning just like all my travels have been!" Jesus figures he still has two-to-three days journey even if he heads straight to Ashod with the way things are going, though he may not be there for quite some time. The shoreline welcomes him back, and he follows its meandering, not thinking where he is headed because the shore will guide him.

Lost in his prayer and thoughts, Jesus quickly covers ten miles or so at a steady pace. Noticing vultures circling in the distance. He remembers his last encounter with those birds and Eli. He decides a little diversion will be welcome and heads that way although apprehensive about what he might find.

Some of the big birds seem concentrated in a group of trees on top of a small rise of rocks. As Jesus approaches to within sling range, he sends a rock flying, which bounces off the trunk of a tree. The vultures take off to join their brothers in flight. He draws near to the group of trees and immediately notices something not right among them. The closer he gets, the more the sight shocks his senses.

He cannot believe what he sees! No wonder the vultures are gathered here! Before him hangs the body of a man! Even from a distance, Jesus notices the bright-blue sash that serves as the rope. The body slightly sways from the breeze coming inland from the sea. Jesus nears the figure, and the smell of rotten flesh attacks his senses, gagging him.

He also notices the misshapen expression on the man's face frozen in death, eyes bulging and terribly swollen. Jesus cannot imagine what might have driven this man to this end. When suddenly he gets a sense he may find the answer to that in Ashod. He notes the location and some landmarks to give proper directions and then sets about doing the unenviable task of taking the body down and providing some sort of burial.

This will at least protect the body from scavenging animals. Before he takes the body down, he digs a shallow grave in the sand and gathers sufficient rocks to stack upon the burial site. This compelled Jesus to consider his next task carefully. While the man was certainly not large in any way, Jesus knows it still will be a major undertaking for him to move the body once on the ground. He knows he must get close to the decaying body to perform this task. There is a large rock slightly behind the body. Jesus surmises it was this rock the man must have stood upon while he fastened the sash around the branch and then his neck.

Jesus steps up and reaches out to untie the sash from the neck. Free from the blue-sash garrote, the body unceremoniously crashes to the ground. But not before it performs a grotesque pirouette as the feet make contact with the earth and lands swollen face up.

Seemingly, it stares wide-eyed into Jesus's own face! He shudders at the sight. Before leaving the rock, Jesus stretches to reach the branch where the sash holds tight from above. Undoing the loop, he lets the sash flutter to the ground. It rests next to the body and flutters no more. Jesus sets to the task. He wishes this part to be over as quickly as possible. Dragging the body to the shallow grave. he rolls it into the trench. Thoughtfully, he covers it with sand and then with rocks. He looks at the gravesite satisfied that his duty is fulfilled to this stranger.

He retrieves the scriptures from his pack and finds the psalms of David. Jesus begins reading aloud chapter 91, "He who dwells in the shelter of the Most High will rest in the shadow of the Almighty. I will say of the Lord, He is my refuge and my fortress, my God, in whom I trust."

After speaking the entire chapter, Jesus looks heavenward, into the blueness of the afternoon sky. He tarries there as the sun soaks into his pores and then concludes with, "Let everything that has breath praise the Almighty!" Jesus takes one last look around the burial site and sees the blue sash resting on the ground. He picks it up and can still smell the odor of death upon it. Perhaps someone will recognize this piece of clothing, so he decides to bring it along.

But now he must attend to himself. He heads back to the seashore and finds a nice warm water shallow section to bathe in. Removing his sandals and outer garments, Jesus wades into the crystal-clear waters. He sits in knee-deep water and is instantly refreshed!

He begins washing and wringing out his clothes and the sash. Soon, the dirt and grime are swept away by the surrounding water. Jesus feels renewed. He gathers the clothes and wades back to shore to fashion a clothes drying rack from sticks. When completed, the rack also serves as shelter from the sun with the clothes drying above. Jesus stretches out beneath the clothes rack and drifts off in a satisfying much deserved afternoon nap.

The sounds of gulls and their irritating calls bring Jesus out of his nap with a start. He props himself up on his elbows and looks around. What he was expecting he does not know and is pleasantly surprised when indeed, he sees nothing except the sun getting very low on the horizon. He sits up quickly and, in so doing, knocks down his makeshift clothes rack. He laughs at himself, but he can't believe his nap has carried him this close to evening!

Well, he thinks, *at least the clothes seem dry.* As he slips them on, he welcomes the clean feeling. Now he feels compelled to make up some time, and in the back of his mind, he *knows* he wants to put some distance between the burial site and himself. Off he goes sea on his right and plains on his left. Jesus figures he can walk for at least two hours before he must find a camp before complete darkness.

Aside from the occasional fishermen, Jesus really hasn't encountered many others on his coastal stroll. If he has seen a fishing village, they all seem to be located inland quite a bit, away from the shore. He supposes that frequent coastal storms are responsible for that.

The women and children he might see as he passes by do not seem at all curious about this lone hiker along the shoreline. Most of the time, Jesus does not mind the separateness and especially not now. However, he soon finds out that YHWH has a different plan for him this evening. As he rounds a slight point no more than 200 yards ahead, there sits a very small fisherman's hut. It is considerably closer to the shore that any other he has come across.

Hmmm, he thinks, *perhaps its location is protected by the point.*

And right away, his presence draws the attention of three small children as they romp around the hut and surrounding beach. Jesus notices that the shoreline has a spot for a boat, but it is not present. He continues walking, and all three children duck inside and soon emerge with a woman. She stands in the doorway, hands on her hips, with three kids attached to her legs, peering from behind.

Her short skirt allows all three a good vantage point. As is his custom, Jesus waves as innocently as possible and continues forward, not wanting to frighten the family. The woman waves back and adds a "come over here" wave at the end.

She beckons to Jesus. He is now even with the hut and no more than seventy feet away and calls, "Hello! My name is Jesus I am on my way south and travel alone. Can I help you with something?"

"Yes! Please, please come here!" she answers. Jesus feels compelled to move closer. As he does, he notices a couple of things. The woman is very pretty and petite, and the three little ones hanging on her legs all seem to be dark-haired girls. The oldest looks to be five or six.

He smiles broadly as he stands before the doorway and family. The woman has not left the safety of the entry to her home. "The gods be praised!" she exclaims. "Just this morning, I prayed for help for my son, my only son!" As she speaks, she glances over her shoulder in reference to the lad hidden inside the dark of the dwelling.

"Are you a physician or healer? Surely, you are the answer to my prayers!" As she looks into the face of this smiling man before her, a keen sense of calm sweeps over her mother's spirit. She instantly recognizes the inner strength of Jesus and that he is not a threat to her or her children. She feels completely safe in his presence.

"I am a Nazarene and simply do the will of my Heavenly Father who has sent me," says Jesus. "What is it that you require of me?"

At that, the woman beckons him into the dwelling saying, "Come, please come in, Jesus the Nazarene." She retreats into the confines of the small home, all the little girls in tow. "A Hebrew huh? I don't think I've ever met a Hebrew before. We don't get many people passing by here. My husband is gone out to sea most of the time, and it is just me and the little ones to fend for ourselves. Sometimes I wish I had my sister here with me, but she lives in Ashod, and I never see her."

She continues as Jesus looks around the sparsely furnished hut. "By the way, my name is Adah. My son Levi, my oldest, has taken a bad turn. He stepped on a puffer fish and is sick unto death. I prayed and prayed that God would send someone to aid us. And now you are here!"

Jesus, in the meantime, has laid eyes on Levi who lies on a woven mat at the back of the hut. Levi does not move. Jesus can see very shallow breathing and sweat beads running from his forehead and face drenching the bed beneath. He also sees the boy's left leg badly swollen and discolored with poisonous tendrils radiating upward through his body.

Jesus winces when he sees the misshapen leg and knows it must be very, very painful. He looks at the woman and sees her pleading eyes. He doesn't bother asking for her permission to go to the boy. As he kneels, he says, "Get me a water-filled cloth that he may sup."

She hurries to get fresh water and a cloth. Jesus reaches and tenderly lifts Levi's head from the mat with his left hand and puts the wet cloth to his lips with his right hand. He squeezes the cloth ever so gently as it touches the boy's lips. This seems to bring Levi out of his feverish stupor, slightly. Levi opens his eyes, a slit revealing steely gray eyes. Jesus cannot help but smile at this response!

"Well, hello there, Levi!" Jesus whispers. "The God YHWH of the Hebrews has sent me so that you may once again be whole."

"Your mother's faith has healed you this day."

Jesus feels Adah very close behind, and although he has whispered to Levi, he knows she too has heard. Jesus turns and stands, and in so doing, notices she has had a hold of the hem of his garment. Her head is bowed as she sobs softly.

Jesus reaches down and places his finger under her chin raising her face. Tears streak her cheeks and droplets land quietly on the sandy floor. Jesus peers intently into her eyes. "Woman, today your faith has healed your house! The grace of YHWH has shined upon you! Your son is healed! By the morning light, Levi will stand and walk completely restored."

The woman cried aloud, "Great is the God YHWH and the Son He has sent!"

Jesus reveled in this praise too. "Woman, no earthly means has revealed this to you see to it that you tell no one what I have done here tonight."

The mother attends to Levi who now sits up on one elbow on the mat. Jesus welcomes the chance to entertain the little girls and is soon engaged in laughing, holding, and bouncing. Each child vies for the attention and touch of this stranger. He is a stranger no more. Jesus notes the sun has completed its course for this day. The fading light signals the eventide. The woman too has noticed this and insists that Jesus stay for dinner. Jesus concedes, looking forward to a simple meal of dried fish, unleavened bread, and cool water from a spring behind the hut.

The merriment around the evening meal is due entirely to the presence of this Nazarene. And it too quickly ends. The girls are all quiet now asleep on their mats. Levi is resting comfortably with the fever broken and poison leaving his leg and body. Adah is busy putting things from the day back in their place, and Jesus is preparing to leave them.

She looks up and sees his preparations and understands he must go. Jesus turns around as he nears the doorway. The woman waves from across the room and turns back to her duties, more to hide the tears than to stay busy. He passes through the doorway and seals the flap behind.

Jesus takes a couple of steps into the night, removes his bedroll, and lays it on the ground in front of the entrance. Like the shepherd watching his flock, he has found his camp in the darkness. Jesus cannot remember a more restful and peaceful sleep. The new dawn finds him all packed, and he strides to the shore. As his foot touches the sea, he glances back to see Adah standing in the door. She waves one last time and turns away back to her family.

Jesus smiles. This test-and-travel session he has experienced since leaving Nazareth has been amazing. Each twist and turn, each relationship and experience have all been provided by the Father. These things further deepen his understanding of what lay ahead— the present and coming darkness, his calling.

Jesus is pretty sure he can make it to Ashod if all goes well today, and he sets his mind to that end. He has no idea what to expect once in Ashod, but if the journey thus far is any indication, then it will be interesting to say the least! Jesus walks and walks and soon begins seeing the telltale signs of a looming civilization. Foot traffic of all sorts abounds. There are walkers and hikers, caravans, carts, and animals being led and ridden alike. The ship and boat traffic is getting heavier near shore and out. He is still three miles away from Ashod and already this much activity! He can only wonder what the city must be like.

Jesus reaches the seaport for Ashod and now must turn east to head for the city. He will fall in line with many other travelers as they unload from ships and boats and arrive from further south even. He is soon lost in small groups of people all heading the same direction. Very few seem to be heading west away from the city. And suddenly there it is! The west gate of the city of Ashod appears in the distance.

The gates stand open wide, inviting one and all to enter. Jesus approaches to within fifty yards of the opening, and he stops. It seems to yawn, like a gapping toothless mouth, ready to gobble up all who enter. He feels the twisted, perverse, anticipation of the people who willingly enter. He certainly is not one of those.

He has completed this trek, and in his mind, Jesus now stands at the gateway to perdition. He shudders as his feet move forward toward the city gate. "Father, strengthen me!"

Entering Ashod

All around Jesus, the people entering through the gate seem in an excited hurry. They pass him by bumping and jostling him as he walks a steady pace, going nowhere in particular. Jesus has planned on seeing the city on his own for a bit before trying to find Cris and Daani's whereabouts. He has never been in a place with so much going on! Oh, he's seen Jerusalem before and other Hebrew cities and villages, but nothing even close to the opulence and ongoing rush as evident here in Ashod.

Jesus is not aware that he has entered through the busiest gate. He soon follows the flow of the crowd toward the center of the city. He notices a small area with a welcoming shade tree and sits beneath it out of the hustle. This will be a perfect spot to watch people and have a timely drink and a bit to eat.

As he gets comfortable, the first thing he notices is the din! People and animals and carts and musical instruments all muddled together in unrecognizable noise! He is glad he is not part of it and takes a deep breath. He sips sweet water dipped from behind the fisherman's family hut. He trusts that family is back to normal by now. He smiles.

And just for a moment, right in the middle of all this clamoring, Jesus thanks YHWH for all the blessings he has been a part of and has received. He realizes the brightest and best sometimes happen right after the darkest and worse. And upon his lips ring, "Sing to the Lord, you saints of His; praise His holy name. For His anger lasts only a moment, but His favor lasts a lifetime; weeping may remain for a night, but rejoicing comes in the morning" (Psalm of David 30:4–5).

Jesus could not help but close his eyes and lift his face heavenward as he recited the scripture. Even in the midst of all this hubbub, someone has noticed the lone figure beneath the shade tree resting in prayer. As Jesus opens his eyes, before him stands a small young woman in plain dress. She is looking intently into his eyes and smiles when their eyes meet.

"Excuse me. Hello! I'm so sorry to intrude, but I noticed you sitting here alone. It looked like you were in prayer or something as I walked up. I find it strange that you would be praying here. Most people pray inside the temple after giving their sacrifice."

She continues on, not letting Jesus comment, "You must not be from around here I guess. Maybe not even a Philistine, huh?" She continues to size Jesus up as she speaks and is not shy about looking him over.

Jesus has gotten to his feet during the woman's prying and stands comfortably under her scrutiny. Jesus finally catches a chance to speak and says, "Woman, out of all the people going to and fro here, you have chosen me to speak with. Why do you suppose that is?" He grins broadly at his own forwardness.

She stutters, "Why, I...I don't know! I guess you looked interesting or lonely or something like that!" In Hebrew society, it is uncommon for a woman to approach a stranger, especially a man. But then again Jesus recalls he is no longer in Nazareth.

"Please, please, come and sit with me. You can share my water and food," Jesus offers, motioning for her to sit. Now that Jesus has spoken and addressed the woman, she feels much more comfortable.

There is just something about this guy that puts you at ease, she thinks.

"Why thank you, sir! I think I will sit with you for a while. Besides, you have a great spot, out of the flow." She comes closer and sits across from Jesus. For a fleeting moment, this interaction has caused the roar of life around them to cease.

With a smile on his face, Jesus begins, "So, woman, what is it that you would like to know about this stranger that prays beneath a tree?"

The woman is relieved that Jesus is receptive and asks, "Who or what were you praying to? Which god? Is there a statue in its shape? I must know! It is just that you looked so...so peaceful and content."

Jesus again smiles. "My name is Jesus, son of Joseph and Mary. I am a Nazarene, from the land of Judah to the north. I am a servant of the Most High God, YHWH."

The woman takes notice of this and says, "Oh, you are a Hebrew! What are you doing here in Ashod? We don't see many Hebrews here, but I do know of a few."

"That is right, woman," Jesus offers. "I am a Hebrew."

Jesus thinks he may have another bit of information that will strike a recognizable chord and offers, "You may recall in the days of our forefathers when the Philistines captured the Hebrew ark in battle." She nods in recollection. "The Ark was brought into the temple of Dagon. Its presence in your land caused great harm to the Philistine people, and the image of Dagon was destroyed by YHWH."

She acknowledges, "Indeed, it is written as you say!"

"I pray to this very God, my Father!" Jesus answers. "He has sent me to prepare His kingdom here on earth when the time is fulfilled." Jesus looks about to see if they are still alone and leans in close to the woman as if to tell a secret, a smile on his face. He says, "I am the Father's servant until my time is revealed, then I will be made known as His Son!"

The woman scoots back a bit at this statement, wide-eyed. Jesus smiles once more as he knows she does not understand exactly what has taken place in this exchange.

Jesus continues with, "So you know that I speak the truth, I will tell you this. You are with child and you will be blessed with a girl. Your husband recently was killed. Your sister, Adah, prays for your visit and certainly could use your help. Adah and her husband will welcome you into their home. Now is the best time for you to leave Ashod and never return."

She is astonished! This stranger knows so much about her. *How could this be?*

Jesus continues, "I do not have much, but please take this coin. It will help you in your preparation for travel to your sister's house on the coast."

He reaches inside his waistband and takes out the only coin he carries and hands it to the overwhelmed weeping woman. She reaches out her hand, and Jesus grasps it in his. He places the coin in it and folds her fingers over it.

"How...how did you know? My name is Adar, and Adah is my twin sister! I miss her so!"

Jesus smiles with a heavenly twinkle in his eye and says, "Yes, I know. I know! You will have much to talk about with your sister."

"Truly, you are a man sent from God!" exclaims Adar.

She regains her composure and asks, "Does this man of God have any place to stay on his first night in Ashod? I do not have much, but my husband at least left me a humble place to stay. You are welcome to stay with me, but be forewarned. The people will talk!"

Jesus smiles broadly at this suggestion and simply says, "Thank you, I will follow where you lead."

Adar and Jesus head back amongst the crowds and disappear into them. They head for the south part of town and must pass by the temple. Jesus will get his first glimpse of the building and see firsthand the goings on in the surrounding streets.

As they navigate the streets, the crowds noticeably get thicker. And then the center of Ashod looms. The temple of Dagon stands without a doubt. Jesus halts to take in this man-made spectacle. The temple colonnade rises before, with splendid columns evenly spaced about a man's arm width apart. It is funny Jesus thinks, *They haven't changed this design even after Sampson destroyed a Dagon temple with this very feature!*

There are thirteen steps stretching along the entire length of the portico. Behind the columns is a large flat porch area leading to the entrance archway. Two temple guards stand, one on each side of the archway. The doorway leading inside stands open, allowing the passersby a glimpse within to the first court. This door remains open during the day and most of the night to encourage worshippers to enter.

There are statues of things that have never walked this earth and many that have. Jesus spies a half-man half-fish statue that seems more prominent that the others and more plentiful.

This must be Dagon itself unmoving, Jesus notices.

His eyes have seen enough. and his heart has no room for the degradation of the human spirit represented here. They move along, headed around the east side of the temple. Immediately, the trinket vendors and sacrifice salesmen overwhelm the airwaves. Calling and shouting, beating drums, and blowing horns—every one of them invading his senses. Each purveyor touts the value of their wares as a direct line to Dagon's favor.

Jesus flinches at the assault. Then he notices each peddler has people lined up waiting to purchase whatever is for sale, willingly laying their money down. As they make their way through the crowds, winding between the hordes, Jesus notices a tent, larger and more ornate than the others. Within and behind a table stands a strikingly handsome woman, dressed in a beautiful flowing garment. She stands adorned with gold and jewels and jet-black hair.

What she sells, Jesus just catches an inkling of.

Jesus does not falter in his stride, but as their eyes meet, a stony pall flashes across her face. Jesus has seen this coldness before and recognizes its source. Her hollow smile burrows through the back of his head as they continue toward Adar's place. Adar approaches a simple dwelling out of the main flow of the crowds. Jesus thinks this will be much quieter and is happy about that. They enter through a single door in a wall without windows. The coolness inside the dwelling immediately embraces the pair, a welcome respite from the heat.

Adar lights a candle, and darkness retreats to the far corners of the room. A warm glow lights the sparse interior. A single table and two chairs, a small fire pit in the wall, and a woven bed mat on a wooden frame are illuminated. A small kitchen area with earthen cups and bowls sitting atop a tiny wooden table sits beneath a window no bigger than two hands. A single wooden laver filled with water sits atop the main table.

Adar says, "I am sorry that I cannot offer you more, but what I have is yours." She smiles meekly.

Jesus responds, "I am used to the night air, open sky, and uneven earth for my bedroll. This will do marvelously. Thank you!"

Adar begins with, "I have recently been widowed. My husband was killed by robbers south of Ashod a month ago. They stole everything he had and left him dead for others to find. I am alone now."

As she fights back the tears, she says, "I will begin my journey to Adah's tomorrow. Ashod holds nothing for me now. I know I can find a trustworthy caravan going that way. Your coin should buy my safety to her home."

"It is a good plan, and YHWH will be your guide along the way," Jesus reassures. "I will help you pack to leave and go with you to the marketplace to find a caravan. The sooner, the better."

It doesn't take long for her few items to be gathered and bound. As the afternoon sun swings westward, they are out the door and headed to the marketplace. As they walk along, Adar offers, "Jesus please stay at the room for as long as you are in Ashod on your visit. You will have it to yourself and be free to come and go as you please. It will at least give you a place to lay your head."

Jesus thinks this is a wonderful idea and gracious offer and accepts. "Thank you. You are most kind."

They soon are among the farmers and livestock and merchant traders. This is a much different setting than they found surrounding the temple. It does not take long to find a merchant preparing a trip north, and Adar's passage is arranged. They will leave in the morning at first light. Jesus assures the leader that Adar and her things will be there on time.

The next morning, Jesus shoulders the bound goods, and they head back to the market in the waning darkness. Adar sits with her goods in the front of a cart pulled by a donkey. She will be riding today. They are a part of the merchant's family caravan. There are three other travelers with carts. *A safe number for travelling*, Jesus thinks. As they prepare to leave, Adar calls Jesus over and hugs him and kisses his cheek. A solitary tear races down her cheek.

Then they move out. Jesus stands still as the noise of the new day pushes the separateness of the moment away. The sun peeks from behind the buildings on the east side of Ashod. Already there are people out and about in the coolness of the morning. Jesus decides to be one of them for the moment. His mission will be to see the entire city and put some inquiries out about Cris and Daani. His heart's cry is that they are no longer even in Ashod. But he knows better and resigns himself to that fact.

Ashod

The Philistine city is laid out so that each of the four exterior gates align to a compass point—north, south, east, and west. The west gate is the entry from the seaport and sees the most traffic. Most vendors and merchants enter through the west gate. Each main street points to the center of town.

In the center stands the temple of Dagon. The temple is situated in the same manner to align with the compass points. The main temple entrance faces north and is the only entrance that is made known and accessible to temple goers. There are other entrances, but only a chosen few know of and use them.

The main employer of the city is the temple. Next in importance are the inns offering rooms, food, and drink. The farmers and trade merchants keep all the staples flowing and also provide high-quality goods to the temple merchants. They then sell them as sacrifice items.

The only appropriate sacrifice is one that has been purchased from the temple merchants. None other is acceptable. The entire focus of the city is to get people, whether travelers or natives, to visit the temple.

Sheba

The days and weeks following Daani and Cris's return to Ashod with the girls have done nothing but solidify their notoriety in the eyes of the townspeople and temple patrons. And most importantly, in the eyes of Sheba!

Daani has healed nicely and is no worse for the wound and has taken to wearing the sword in his belt. A prominent display of death-defying heroics indeed! It certainly adds to the intimidation factor. Cris has taken all the attention in stride and is Cris! Sheba has come to realize how fortunate she is to have these faithful and willing young men at her side to do her bidding. She will do whatever it takes to protect her power over them. Her jealousy is savage, and many have felt its fury! Sheba has her finger on the pulse of the city of Ashod.

Rarely, if ever, does a traveler who stays for an extended visit not pass her scrutiny. And so it is with the likes of the Hebrew visitor Jesus. He came to her attention not long after Adar left and he began staying at her place. She doesn't know much out about this guy though and has no idea of the connection between Jesus, Cris, and Daani. As far as she knows, this guy is from Nazareth; Cris and Daani are from Bethlehem. If she had known their history, she surely would have done everything in her power to see that Jesus left quietly, without hooking up with his old friends.

As far as she was concerned, he was just another Jew in search of all the physical pleasures that Ashod had to offer. Sheba was sure she would be seeing Jesus at the temple in no time at all. She may be right on that account but not in the manner she thinks.

Sheba was well aware of all the stories being circulated of the prophet in the wilderness and the miracles and intercessions that have reportedly taken place. This guy was becoming famous in the region, and people were more than willing to share their wilderness encounter with him. There was no way that she would have ever imagined that this inauspicious young Hebrew man was the one who the travelers were speaking of. It never crossed her mind.

Then there was her working relationship with Cris and Daani. For the most part, they could come and go as they wish. If they were summoned to Sheba's side or the temple, they immediately would cease whatever they were doing and head there on a trot. They were always at her beck and call and never more than a few minutes away from her side at any time. Of course, there were the temple guards that would come instantly to her side in an emergency, but by, far Sheba preferred the company of her "boys." She told them often of that fact, and they always enjoyed hearing her say so.

No Chance Meeting

This day was like many in the past and promised more of the sameness. Daani and Cris didn't mind that one bit as they walked the city streets, just showing themselves—no crisis, no emergency, no problems. This suits them just fine.

While they were tied into the same grapevine that Sheba has access to, they didn't pay as much attention to all details about individuals as she did. If someone came to their attention, it was because Sheba told them to take note. So they were really surprised as one day they rounded a corner, and within their sight was a stranger. This stranger had an old familiar air about him, though.

His dress was familiar. His build and demeanor were familiar. His mannerisms, as he conversed, were familiar. All these familiarities came from their memories of many years past. But they were looking at a grown man across the way. They stood out of this man's sight to better size him up and see if the familiarity held up under their scrutiny.

Unadorned traditional Hebrew garb for travel hangs loosely, falling to the handmade sandals. A shepherd's sling hangs from his belt. He has long, wavy brown hair just touching the shoulders. Sun-darkened skin covers his face, hands, and legs and any skin exposed.

Daani looks at Cris and says, "He sure looks like Jesus."

Cris says, "That he does. Everything about him brings back memories of the last time we saw him. It has to be Jesus!" With minds made up, they waste no time in closing the distance to where Jesus is talking with a shopkeeper. As Cris and Daani approach, the shopkeeper looks over Jesus's shoulder and sees the duo. He abruptly cuts off the conversation and backs away to give the approaching thugs some regard.

Jesus notices the change in the keeper's posture and turns to see who approaches. In doing so, he faces the morning sun and just sees the shapes of two men. Jesus raises his hand to shade his eyes, and Cris and Daani realize they have the advantage of the sun and skirt to the side of Jesus to help clear his vision.

They stop and wait for Jesus to focus and offer some kind of recognition, and it comes almost instantly! Jesus's face lights up! The surprised and joyous expression is contagious, and Cris and Daani grin broadly. The three embrace like long-lost brothers! Cris and Daani pound on Jesus's back. Jesus slaps them each on the shoulders. What a wonderful moment!

Their voices intermingle as they all talk at once. "You look great!"

"When did you get here?"

"You haven't changed a bit!"

Time stood still and then reversed its course. Running, laughing, scrapes and bruises, false bravado—the hide! It all came flooding back as the reality of the moment faded away—dim, dimmer, gone.

And for a brief instant, they were seven years old again. Differences didn't matter. Social status didn't matter. Ideology didn't matter. All that mattered was that they were united again in time and space. And then time rights itself as it always does.

The moment flees. The instant vanishes. The feelings consume themselves. The now returns. Far too quickly, the reality of the surroundings come back into focus and obliterate the fantasy of remembrance. The smile that is stuck to their faces begins to whither like unwatered crops. And all that can be offered is a time to sit, reflect, and share.

But for that fleeting initial jubilation, there would be none. At arm's length now the trio stands. Daani offers continuation, saying, "Lets head over to Ben's inn and get something to eat and drink so we can talk!"

Cris agrees, "Sounds like a great idea. Let's go!"

Jesus follows as they head into the morning rush and are soon lost in the crowds. As he looks at his two best friends in the world walk ahead, he observes a couple of things. As they approached, others in the street, the people, move out of the way. Jesus sometimes senses resentment in some of the people as they relinquish the right of way. Cris and Daani walk with a confidence that is present in each step. They are both dressed very well in clean clothes and clean bodies. Cris's well-defined physique is not hidden completely beneath his loose clothing, and Daani looks trim and fast. The sword present in Daani's waistband completes the picture of self-assuredness in the pair. Jesus observes they are quite a pair, quite a pair indeed!

They arrive at Ben's place and take a seat among the rest of the patrons. Ben sees them sit down and immediately comes over to their table, smiling broadly. He always is glad when Cris and Daani are present, the whole inn just seems to run smoother.

"Good to see you. What'll it be today, boys?" Ben asks. He turns to Jesus and, in the same breath, asks, "And who is your friend here?"

Jesus starts to answer, but Daani doesn't give him a chance and jumps in, "This is our old friend Jesus. We all grew up together in Bethlehem as kids. We haven't seen him for quite a few years now. We just ran into him in town this morning!"

Cris offers, "Yeah, it's like the old days, all three of us together again! Bring us some new wine and some of your best bread—the good stuff, Ben!"

Ben acknowledges and turns to walk away with the order on his mind, takes a step, and turns back, looking at Jesus. "Did you say your name was Jesus? Is that right? Jesus?"

Jesus smiles and laughs and says, "Well, I actually didn't say, but yes, my name is Jesus."

Bens spins on his heel to fill the order and mutters to himself as he walks through the other tables, "Jesus, now where have I heard that name before?"

Jesus looks at his friends closely and notes out loud, "You two look great. You must have found life in Ashod to your liking. I heard about what happened in Bethlehem and all. Seems like you guys got the bad end of that deal."

Daani says, "Yeah, we left that place as soon as we got out of jail and have never gone back. I do miss my mom, though. I should have sent for her a long time ago. I don't even know if she is alive."

Cris too remembers the pain and suffering of their last days in Bethlehem and chooses to not speak of them. The melancholy subdues them all for a moment. And then Ben appears with the bread and drink, breaking the depression and offering a chance to change subjects, a welcome change.

And then Ben does it for them. "Jesus huh?" Ben blurts, "You said your name was Jesus. I knew I heard that name before! You are the guy that people are talking about meeting in the wilderness north of here. You are doing all the healings and miracles and all that, right? Are you are some kind of a prophet?"

Jesus tries to deflect the comment and simply asks, "People have said these things and you believe them?"

Ben answers, "Well yeah, I guess. I don't know!"

"I am a servant of the Most High God, my Father, the God of our father Abraham, the Hebrew God YHWH," Jesus says this looking directly into Ben's eyes. "I am here to simply do my Father's bidding."

This is way too much information for Ben, and he turns and heads back to the kitchen, shaking his head. His departure leaves at least two at the table sitting staring at the food, not saying a word.

Jesus understands the silence and offers, "I have not come all this way to talk about hearsay. I want to know what you two have been up to and what you are doing now! You must be doing well. You look so good!"

With that, both of his old comrades look up, again ready to reminisce and share. Cris starts, "When we left Bethlehem, we were pretty upset and hurt. We thought that Ashod might have something to offer, and we came here. We have found steady work and gotten to know a lot of people in the city. We work for a woman named Sheba. She runs the temple of Dagon and most of the city. She knows everything and everybody, and we work for her."

Daani cuts in, saying with a smile, "Yeah, she takes real good care of us! We have a real nice place to stay, and all the money and everything we could ever want or need, she gives to us."

Jesus looks a little surprised at Daani's comment and says, "She gives to you? What do you do for her? What is your job?"

"Well, we do whatever she needs done!"

Cris stops Daani at that and offers simply, "We fix problems she has with people and payments to the temple. We help her make sure the city runs smoothly. We take care of whatever needs taking care of. You know, we make her problems disappear!"

"I see," Jesus says. "You two and this woman, Sheba, you know a lot about what goes on in this city and these parts, huh?"

"Yes, I guess you could say that," Cris offers.

"Well, then, perhaps you might know something about this," and Jesus reaches into his shirt and pulls out the bright-blue sash that he took off the hanging man. He lays it on the tabletop. "I found this on a man that had hanged himself in the desert about twenty miles north of here. I can't imagine what would have driven him to do that. But nonetheless, it was done. I took him down and buried him near where I found him. I would like to tell someone in the city where he is buried in case anyone knows who he is."

At the sight of the bright-blue sash, they both catch their breath. They listened to what Jesus says before exhaling. Daani speaks, "Hung himself, huh? That is pretty sad. Yeah, we know who that belonged to. He wasn't a very good guy. He tried to kill his own daughters. We saved them."

Well, that is kind of what happened, Daani thinks to himself.

Cris chimes in with, "Yeah, Daani took the sword blade hit in the back, saving the girls' lives. It is the very sword he carries in his belt!"

Continuing on, Cris says, "We know just who to tell about what you found and where the body is. We'll take care of it from here, thanks."

He picks up the blue sash and hands it to Daani, who in turn ties it in a loop and hangs it loosely across his shoulder and chest. That being said and done, they begin sharing the wine and bread.

Jesus takes the lead and relates his simple life of the past six years. He begins with leaving Nazareth. He tells of finding his spiritual guidance in dreams and revelations from YHWH. He tells of his travel by foot and living alone in the desert. The four years spent with Eli and his relationship with this old prophet. Jesus tells them of how he finally comes to fully understand his connection with the heavenly realm, with God the Father and his purpose on this earth. Jesus concludes with a full disclosure to his friends, "The world is not yet ready for the revelation of the chosen One, God's only Son. The Messiah. That will be when my work here on earth really begins. Until that time, I do His work and reflect His glory. The stories you hear of relationships and healings and miracles are but a glimpse of the salvation that will come at the dawning of my ministry."

"You will be challenged to choose, and choose you must. You will be required to declare your allegiance to the Living God or to man. Your salvation will depend upon it." Cris and Daani have sat and listened to all that Jesus has related to them. They struggle with their boyhood memories and rubbing shoulders with this man that now would be "Messiah."

How can this be? They know of his human frailties. They know of his parents. The real confusion comes because they really do know he is extraordinary and always has been! But this! All this is so hard to fathom! To understand! To comprehend! Jesus senses their disbelief and wonderment and offers this, "Do not just hear the words that my Father speaks through me, but do them. If I do not do what my Father tells me to do, what kind of a son am I?"

Jesus says, "Watch what I do in my Father's name, and make your choice. I cannot make the choice for you." Jesus has defined his agenda and his ultimate purpose on this earth, and quite frankly, it makes his friends squirm.

Both Cris and Daani think it is quite one thing to hear others tell of these stories and then discount them. It is entirely another thing to have Jesus here with them relating the stories. There is something about Jesus that makes you want to listen closely. The heavy talking is over for now, and they soon drift into small talk. This allows them to momentarily ignore the major differences of their divergent lives.

The morning ends all too soon, but it is perfect timing as they run out of small talk. Cris and Daani must return to their routine, and Jesus has some exploring on his own he wants to do. They agree to meet again in the evening.

Death in Ashod

Jesus thinks he will head to the center of town and watch the people around the temple, and Jesus does just that. He meanders his way through the crowds, looking, watching, and listening. It is well after high noon as he approaches the front steps of the temple. There seems to be a commotion brewing on the porch just outside the archway, and Jesus climbs to the seventh step and stops to watch.

A man is yelling back into the temple as he is being physically removed by two of the temple guards. The man is fighting with each step and is screaming about being robbed by a servant girl of the temple. The guards are becoming quite animated and agitated with his behavior. And then Jesus sees her. She stands just outside of the archway, closely watching the work of the guards, the darkness of the inner temple chamber behind her.

She is a beautiful woman dressed in a silk gown. Her jet-black hair glistens in the reflected sun. Ivory and gold and silver adorn her clothing and is woven into her hair. *This must be Sheba,* Jesus thinks, as he too is taken with her beauty and presence for an instant.

She yells to the guards trying to contain the unruly man. "He is no longer welcome here! The temple doors will no longer welcome him! Leave this place and never return!" She screams and points in the air, past Jesus toward the north gate of the city. Many others have taken notice of this outburst and now stand in rapt attention.

The guards are renewed in strength by the impetuous of Sheba's voice and gesture. They restore their efforts to drag the screaming, cursing man and finally throw him down the steps. He tumbles toward Jesus and stops his roll on skinned-and-bloody knees.

Blood also covers his hands and face. He stops on the very step Jesus now occupies. Jesus has remained standing still during this entire episode and now calmly looks into the wild eyes of this humiliated man. The man looks into Jesus's face, and Jesus calmly says to him words he has already heard but with a very different meaning this time, "Leave this place and never return."

Immediately, Jesus notices a peaceful spirit of understanding come across the man's bloodied face. In an instant the calming spirit vanishes when from atop the steps comes unabashed, mean laughter. Above the ridiculing chorus rises a cackle; a woman's piercing cadence. This lilt cuts deep to the quick of the bloodied man's pride. As anger spurs prides' response the man charges up the highest six steps on a dead run toward the archway; which amplifies the sound and is the source of his torment. A short blade, once hidden in his sandal is now clenched in his right hand. Jesus stands motionless, unable to do anything but watch as human discord takes center stage. The woman has turned away from the steps and has her arms around the shoulders of the two triumphant guards. They continue laughing as they walk toward the archway, toward darkness.

Sheba is unaware of the assassin on a dead run for her. Her laughter, his target. The bloodied man's rage has narrowed his vision. He quickly closes the distance sure now of his target in noon daylight. The trio passes beneath the archway about to enter the dimness of the chamber when a flash is seen in the corner of Sheba's eye. A blur with a tint of bright blue!

Sheba whirls just in time to see Daani intercept the bloodied man's enraged charge. And with the swiftness of a snake's strike, Daani buries the sword to the hilt in the bloodied man's midsection! The man's charge is cut short in midstride by the speed of the blade. Daani, out of breath and shaking, leans forward, hands on his knees, wavering over the twitching body.

The bright-blue sash hangs loosely across his chest, dangling underneath. Cris is a second behind and now stands over the prone dead man. His fists clenched tightly, ready if needed. Cries arise and are carried upon the wind intermingled with screams and gasps. People are frozen in place.

171

The only movement seems to come from the growing pool of blood that slowly spreads its wings to full span. Its flight, however, never leaves the ground. Jesus sinks to his knees and weeps. Once again, darkness has shone its face in daylight.

And then the murmuring and whispers and voices begin again. People begin running, either from the scene or to the scene. Chaos ramps up to full speed. The guards feign protecting Sheba and form a perimeter around her, the threat already subdued.

The champions of the moment assess the fallen man and the gathering crowd. They immediately call for more temple guards, "Get the guards! We need to keep these people back! Sheba, are you okay?" Cris is yelling over the growing din.

Sheba pushes past the guards to stand next to the body. She stands with her hands on her hips and surveys the growing crowd. Sensing they expect something from her, she grabs Cris and Daani by the arms and takes a few steps forward. The body lays motionless behind.

Raising her arms above her head and commanding silence, she bellows, "Quiet! Quiet, everyone!" The crowd reluctantly gives her a subdued moment. "What you have seen here today will happen to those who come against the temple of Dagon! Once again, the gods and the protectors of the temple have defeated those that would go against us! Worship at his feet! He requires your sacrifice daily!"

She has full command of the situation at this time. "To remind everyone that enters this chamber of the price of dissent and to those that may come against us, this body will remain in view for three days!"

At that, someone begins chanting, "Dagon! Dagon! Dagon!" Soon, the entire crowd is caught up in the dark mood.

Jesus has heard and witnessed all that he can take for the moment. He now has full insight into the temple and the beast that is its heart. He sees the evil within Sheba for what it is—unquenchable. It pains his very soul recognizing that Cris and Daani are mainstays in this evil pretense.

He must get to a quiet place and seek the Father for wisdom and strength. As he stumbles down the steps, the throng's upheaval reaches a crescendo, and Jesus covers his ears to muffle the madness. It works for a moment, long enough for him to reach the outer wall dwellings. Soon he stands before his temporary home and enters the coolness of the stone walls. His ears continue ringing from the verbal onslaught. Sounds of torment from the dead and the enslaved drown out reason.

He falls to his knees, and his face finds the floor. Jesus cries out, "Abba Father, hear me I pray! I have seen the darkness in the hearts of men! Their willingness to follow any god that promises gratification of their desires is evident in all they do. They pay no mind to the cost of these desires. They serve only one god—the god of darkness, death, and self. Yet I know that there is only YHWH! The Great I Am! Father, the load is great, and the path is uncertain, but I trust in You! Lead me, I pray!"

The stillness breaks through the clamor and cancels all other sounds. Jesus is engulfed by peace—a peace that passes all human comprehension. The Father speaks in the stillness, "Son, do not be discouraged. The great deceiver of nations is in this place. But take heart, the Great I Am has overcome this captor of men's hearts! The Son of God and Son of Man will prevail! You will overcome the world!"

Jesus responds in a hushed voice, "Father, through you, I can accomplish all things!" Jesus remains in prayer and solitude the rest of the day. The coolness in the room is much more welcoming than what he knows he would find in the streets. His compassion for the aimless beings just outside the walls of his room grows and grows as does his understanding of the importance of his presence on earth. He allows the sanctity of the moment to overtake his senses, passing into a welcome slumber.

He awakens with a start and immediately sees a man and a woman standing in the room! He notices fading sunlight from outside and surmises it must be nearing evening. The couple does not speak, nor do they move. At first, Jesus thought it was Cris and Daani returning for the night visit as they had suggested.

Jesus now knows it is not them. Each figure shimmers in the fading light. A hood covers each head. There is form, with no definition, and they are big, larger than any human Jesus has ever seen! Then Jesus notices something else. The two stand inside the entrance with the door behind. It filters in the fading sun's light. They cast no shadows!

The angelic beings bow in unison before Jesus. They remain face down until Jesus rises. "The Father sent us to your side while you slept." The voice seems to come from them both. "Your presence here has not gone unnoticed. The forces of this world have gathered against you in this place. Your time has not yet come to face the evil one. We will see to your welfare until you choose to leave. Anyone with malice in their heart toward you will not be allowed to touch you. We will abide with you until the Father calls us home. We will not leave your side until that time."

Jesus does not know what to say or do. He certainly has not expected these guardians to attend him! Once again, Jesus whispers, "Thank you, Father!" As Jesus stands looking at these two magnificent creations, he sees shadows cross the threshold of the entrance door. The beings effortlessly part—one to the left and one to the right. They instantly melt into the background.

Cris and Daani stand at the door and holler in, "Aren't you going to invite us in?"

Jesus quickly answers, "Sure! Enter! Please come in!"

They enter and cross directly to Jesus and embrace. Once again, the childhood bonds are renewed. "Please, sit down, my brothers," Jesus implores. As they sit ,Jesus remembers what his guardians had just told him and is comforted knowing Cris and Daani where allowed contact with him.

Cris begins as they sit, "Man, what a day! After we met with you this morning, we had an unfortunate incident at the temple."

Jesus looks up and simply says, "Yes, I know. I was there too."

Daani gulps hard and says, "You were there? You saw what happened?" Jesus nods, and Daani continues, "Oh man. I am sorry you had to see that. That was real bad!"

"Indeed," Jesus says as he slowly stands to his feet. "What I witnessed today was man's inhumanity against man. One of the Father's most cherished possessions was cast aside as a service to the evil one."

With sadness upon his face, Jesus continues, "As a matter of fact, you do what is right in your own eyes without considering what is right in the eyes of God. You have forgotten the teachings of our fathers. You have forgotten the scriptures. My heart weeps for you, my brothers. I weep because I see what you have become and what you have forsaken. You think that God has forsaken you, but it is you that have chosen to turn from Him! Soon, there will come a time when men will no longer be able to discern light from dark and good from evil. Listen to what I say!"

"My time has not yet come, but when it arrives, I will seek those with willing hearts to accomplish the Father's and my purpose here on earth. Oh, that you my brothers, would be among those that are so called to do the Father's will. Many will be called, but few will be chosen. Hear this, brothers! Soon I will proclaim the good news to all mankind. I will say the time has finally come and that the kingdom of God draws nigh. When you hear these things of me, repent and believe the good news! Your salvation draws nigh!"

And so it is that Jesus shares the most intimate details of his coming ministry with the two he came to call brothers. Daani and Cris had no idea the truth that Jesus just revealed to them in this guarded exchange. Their eyes were clouded by this present darkness. They could not comprehend the light even though they were in its presence.

Leaving Ashod in Darkness

The time has come for Jesus to end his stay in Ashod. All his hopes and dreams for Cris and Daani dashed upon the rocks of servitude to gods other than Jehovah. Cris and Daani sense an uneasiness within their own souls. The time for Jesus's departure has arrived, and they should just let him go on his way, but the purpose of their visit tonight still rings in their ears.

Sheba has now put the entire story of this man named Jesus together and had sent them to bring him to her side. What she would want with their friend, Jesus, they don't know, but they will do her bidding. "You have spoken to us like the brother that you are," Daani begins, "but our allegiance is to Sheba and the god Dagon. Do not ask us to choose between our love for you and our service to them please! There is plenty of time for that!"

Jesus shudders at Daani's words. He recognizes the futility of the moment and simply hangs his head and says, "Brothers, you have already chosen. My visit here is at an end. Please come with me to the north gate."

"Grant us this one last request before you leave," Cris says. "Sheba wants to meet the one the people all talk about meeting in the wilderness, the Nazarene called Jesus! Can you come with us before you leave?"

"I see no reason to meet with her, but if you wish, I will do it for you," Jesus consents.

The trio leave the humble room Jesus has used for his home and heads into the darkened streets of Ashod. His guides know the streets and corners and pathways like the back of their hands. They glide effortlessly though the growing evening crowds. Jesus still is amazed at the number of people who fill the streets after sundown.

But then he recognizes also that evil loves darkness. A chill runs its bony fingers up his spine. They soon approach the temple area and the front steps. Immediately, Jesus notices the activity around the body of the bloodied man. True to Sheba's words, the body lays in full view of temple patrons. Jesus observes that some don't even notice the deceased as they walk, looking into the allure inside. How sad!

Daani and Cris head up the congested steps toward the entrance, and Jesus stops at the bottom. He will not go further. Daani turns to see Jesus at the bottom of the steps and trots back down to his side. "Come on, Jesus, Sheba is inside the temple."

Jesus stands firm, unmoving and simply says, "I will wait here. If she wants to meet, bring her to me. This is the only way."

At that, Daani turns and trots back up to meet Cris who waits on the platform. "Jesus says he will not go any further. If she wants to talk, Sheba must come out to see him."

Cris shrugs his shoulders and says, "I don't know if she'll go for that, but I'll see."

Across the platform, he goes in search of Sheba. Cris is pretty sure she won't want to leave the temple to talk to Jesus. She would be out of her element, and he senses somehow vulnerable. Cris has no idea how right he is about this cat-and-mouse game he is in the midst of. As Cris enters through the archway, he pauses just long enough to get a picture of the flow inside. This guarded habit has served him well. Everything seems in order, and he advances toward a female temple servant who beams at his approach.

"Well, hello there, Cris! Have you come to see me tonight?" She fusses, hoping for his attention.

Cris smiles and simply says, "Where is Sheba? I need to speak with her." Instantly disenchanted, the woman motions toward the east side of the temple with a flip of her hand. Cris looks at her and says, "Go tell her I am here." The woman obliges and is off in a huff to fetch Sheba.

In a moment, Sheba emerges from a side room and waves for Cris to come over. He sees her and heads to her side. Cris is always taken by the beauty of this woman. Tonight is no exception. She rests easily with her back against the entry of a private chamber. Lamps and candlelight point to the doorway and illuminate her features. *Tonight, she looks stunning, as good as she has ever looked,* Cris thinks.

He smiles as he approaches and notices Sheba looking over his shoulder, past him, as if in anticipation of someone else. "Well, where is he, your friend Jesus? I thought you were bringing him to me!"

"I did. We did! He is here. I mean outside! He said he will meet you outside the temple. He will not come in," Cris stumbles in the explanation.

Sheba laughs devilishly. "He won't come into the temple, huh? What do you suppose he is afraid of, Cris? I thought this guy was a prophet and miracle worker! He can cast out demons and heal the sick. Do you suppose he's afraid of little old me? I sure hope you and Daani don't put too much faith in this guy. Seems to me he's not who he says he is!" She snickers and sinks her talons deeper. "Well, we'll just have to go to him and meet him outside then. I am not afraid to meet him there!"

She reaches out and takes Cris by the arm. Sheba knows very well that Jesus will see this as a personal defeat—she and Cris together. Any advantage she can muster will be helpful. She has already figured this battle would come. Sheba has overlooked and doesn't understand that Jesus has had special insight into this meeting also.

The stage is set. The God of warriors girded about with truth and vision of the past and future! The gods of man girded with deceit and lust and envy with no thought for the future! An unimaginable place for Jesus to be tested.

Sheba's persona changes in the twinkling of an eye! Her vestige hardens. Her stride lacks the feminine purveyance and glide. She walks with a boldness found in soldiers marching in review. Off to confront goodness, she strides reliant on the dark powers that control men's hearts. As they wait, Jesus and Daani stand and watch the people in the night. Free under the cover of darkness to be whomever they wish, the reticence of daylight now removed.

Lurid, spectacular, sultry, inviting, condescending, uninhibited, deviant and diverse, Sheba appears at the top of the steps with Cris on her arm. She stops for a moment, overlooking the movement of the night. She gathers strength from the darkness. The huge oil lamps lining the steps cast a pall, a yellow tint, over objects in their influence.

People and objects alike are affected by the flickering. She steps from her vantage point, and they descend toward Jesus and Daani. Sheba halts on the last step and remains higher, just above Jesus's head in position. This too calculated in her mind as an advantage.

Cris clears his throat as if to introduce the two, and Sheba injects, "Well, well, this must be Jesus, the long-lost friend of my cohorts and confidantes, Cris and Daani!" The condescending voice is not lost on Jesus. Sheba tries to extend her hand to Jesus but somehow is restrained from doing so. It is quite evident to those gathered as she fights the heavenly restraint. In frustration, she relaxes her attempt.

Jesus makes no move to offer his hand in greeting. He stands before Sheba, looking at her with a straight face. He doesn't smile nor does he scowl.

For the moment, the crowd noise, movement, and conversation cease in their circle. Then Jesus speaks, "Yes, I am Jesus of Nazareth born in Bethlehem. Cris and Daani and I sat together under our mother's tutelage as children."

Sheba is somewhat taken aback by Jesus and his calm, restrained demeanor and certainly by the unseen restraint! She has lost some of her puffiness in his presence and asks, "Are you the same man that we have heard about that wanders in the desert and heals the sick and performs other miracles?"

Jesus answers, "It is as you say."

Sheba presses on, "And by whose authority are these things done?"

"I have been sent by my Heavenly Father, YHWH. The Living God of the Hebrew peoples," Jesus states.

At this statement, Sheba inches back. She is well aware of the history that the Philistines have with this Hebrew God, YHWH!

Dagon was destroyed by the presence of the ark of the covenant! And the mighty man of strength, Sampson, destroyed the temple of Dagon by knocking down the pillars after praying to this same Hebrew God!

"Have you come to destroy this temple and city as your God and forefathers have done in times past? Have you come to undermine my power and dominion over these simple-minded slaves? Have you come to prophesy to and disparage the people of Ashod?" She snickers as the dark truth begins to emerge!

"Indeed, this temple will be destroyed but not by my earthly hands," Jesus responds. "These walls will not stand against the coming judgment of the Most High and the Son He has sent. There will not be one stone left upon another in that great day of the Lord!"

"I have seen the great darkness that you peddle. It enslaves the people of this city. You offer fulfillment of their evil desires and allow them to trade their very souls to gratify their human lust!" Jesus is hitting his stride now and continues with, "Woe unto you, woman of perdition! Your path to destruction has already been foretold!"

Sheba could sense the crescendo of Jesus's words even before he spoke them and has already begun retreating up the temple steps before Jesus's last statement. Cris and Daani had been caught up in the exchange and were now caught off guard by the forcefulness of Jesus's statements. Cris does not move up with Sheba and stands with mouth open in shock!

Daani grabs Jesus and puts his arms around him, not to restrain him but simply to try and reason with him by touch. Jesus takes no offense at Daani's embrace and simply looks him in the face knowingly. "Jesus, man, you really got carried away there!"

Cris yells, "I've never heard anyone talk to Sheba like that! It is good for you that you are leaving Ashod. I don't think you would be welcome here any longer!" Looking at Cris and then Daani, Jesus knew it would come to this.

But he still holds out hope for his friends. "I must go as you say, but please come with me! I cannot offer you comfort or prosperity or even a roof over your head or food. But what the Father gives to me,

I give to you. Come, please go with me and leave this place forever!" Jesus pleads.

The pagan temple of Dagon rises behind the trio as Jesus offers a final way out. His words of wisdom fall on deaf ears and hardened hearts. Speaking up, Cris states as a matter of fact, "We will walk with you to the east gate of the city. As for me, I will cast my lot with Ashod and all the things I have come to love in this life. I cannot speak for Daani."

Daani clears his throat and simply says, "We will see you out of the city."

Jesus once again is engulfed in human anguish and turns away from the temple. He resolves to never lay eyes upon it again. Each painful step he takes enlarges the gulf between him and his childhood friends. Jesus trudges forward. Cris and Daani lag a few steps behind. All too soon, the east gate looms mouth gapping at Jesus, ready to disgorge this Son of Man. Jesus keeps walking as he passes under the arch, leaving Cris and Daani dumbfounded that he doesn't stop.

They both run after Jesus! They make him stop as they plant themselves before him, an incredulous, perplexed look on their faces. "Jesus, stop! Please!" They plead in unison!

Jesus stops. "My heart is too heavy to say good-bye. I know that we shall surely meet again, but for the moment, I am suffering the loss of my brothers. I wish that I could change your minds or physically remove you from this place. However, that is a choice you must make. And today, you have chosen to serve man. I will hold out hope for your return to reason and right," Jesus has said all that he is capable of saying.

Daani and Cris stand before him, refusing to part shoulders to let him pass. Jesus steps forward and encircles their necks with his arms. He softly places his head on their shoulders, Daani on his right and Cris on his left.

Amidst the clouds of dust and passersby hurrying to and fro, no one even notices the embrace of the three men. Now his path, his mission, his calling beckons to him from beyond the cast light of the city. In the night it calls. But alas, he does not seem to be able to break the embrace and start down the road to their next and last meeting.

Jesus finally lets go. His mind clears, and Jesus is able to speak, "I have loved you!" These words are all he can muster but certainly enough. Cris and Daani do not speak. The last words have already been uttered. Jesus pushes through the wall of memories and moves into the night, into the darkness of loss. He will never return to Ashod even though the ruins of his heart remain.

Lost in Purpose

The lights and sounds are soon glimmers and murmurs as Jesus trudges into the darkness. His heart has lost its compass for the moment. Clear of the city, Jesus falls to his knees, distraught over the choices his friends have made. It is perhaps the darkest hour his human form has ever endured.

"Father, You know my heart is broken. You are the giver of life and all things good. Establish in me a new spirit now, I pray!" Under the cover of nightfall Jesus moves, unaware of his bearing. He does not look at the stars; he does not seek direction. He proceeds with no mind of course other than moving away from the pitch-black that is Ashod. The morning will offer new hope and direction.

Jesus marches all night. The glowing streaks in the eastern sky let him know that the new morn approaches. According to the rising sun, Jesus has turned south. And that is fine with him. He has never been on a trip to the south, and there is certainly no time like the present! He knows little about the world to the south.

All knowledge he possesses comes from the scriptures and tales of the Hebrew people in days of old. This land represents so much in Hebrew history, and as Jesus sits to rest, he thinks about the days gone by as they are written and passed down from generation to generation—the garden of Eden, Noah and the great flood, Tower of Babel, Father Abraham, Moses and the plagues of Egypt, captivity and freedom, Red Sea, Ten Commandments, forty years in the desert, Sampson, Saul, David and Goliath, Solomon, the temple, conquerors and being conquered.

He smiles to think that his very own travels and ministry will be among those also. All will be written down and spoken of for generations and generations to come even until the end of time! His own legacy is still being formed and enacted by God's very hand, simply amazing and his that is yet to experience!

It is with divine excitement that Jesus begins this portion of discovery. He knows full well that this will lead to the end of his earthly ministry and the complete fulfillment of his divine purpose. Ultimately, he will answer the call to return to the heavenly realm from which he came. So much is left to be done, and so little time is left to do it! Even the Son of Man must contend with human constraints.

And one of them closes in upon him even as he sits—the midday sun! No longer near enough to the shore of the Great Sea to have the comforting daily breeze, the harsh reality of the high desert mountains surround him. Jesus welcomes this challenge once again. He even thinks he may have gotten soft from his stay in Ashod and sleeping on a bed! He breathes deeply as the warmed air fills his lungs. Content he is where he should be for the moment, he smiles to himself and thanks the Father.

Ah, the life of a wanderer once more. Free to come and go, go or stay, walk or run. There will be plenty of demands for his time in the future. Right now, however, it is just the Father, the earth, and the sky! Suddenly now, he grows weary from his travel during the night. A respite from the heat and closing of his eyes would be a welcome intermission. Besides, his mind needs a rest from all he has witnessed in the last couple of days.

Jesus is determined to find a spot for rest and heads up over a small rise in the rocks. At the crest, he spies a formation that should offer shade and flat spot to recline for a time. Indeed, it is the perfect spot. He could not have been napping for more than a couple of hours when he senses movement and hears cloven feet on the rocks. He wakes not in fright but more out of curiosity.

His peering eyes reveal sheep, many sheep. With his movement, Jesus has caused an alarm to run through the flock, and the animals instantly are on edge. Jesus knows how skittish these animals can be and slowly gets to his feet. His appearance in the middle of the herd comes much to the surprise of the shepherd boy in attendance.

Their eyes meet, and there is neither panic nor unease. Wonder is the only emotion either can sense. Common ground has now visually been established, and the shepherd boy waves meekly at Jesus. Jesus, still in the midst of fifty or sixty animals, slowly raises his hand in gesture of friendship, palm out toward the lad.

The boy makes a few clucking noises followed by a low whistle. The lad then taps his shepherds crook against a rock, *click-clack, click-clack.* The sheep instantly respond by moving toward him. This leaves Jesus standing alone in a cloud of sheep dust.

He watches the boy smartly maneuver the herd down the hill toward a crude man-made and natural enclosure. They enter through a gap in some boulders. The entire parade soon vanishes from Jesus's sight, except for the dust cloud that pinpoints their position behind the rocks and bushes.

Jesus has kept his distance. He understands the responsibilities this shepherd boy has toward the protection of his sheep. He will wait for the boy to reappear once he has secured his flock and calmed their nervousness. It doesn't take long for the boy to emerge at the boulder entrance, but his work is not yet complete. He dutifully closes off the opening by dragging some brush across the passageway. Content now that his flock is safe, the boy turns to look for Jesus.

As their eyes meet across the boulder-strewn landscape, Jesus waves a greeting. The boy signals by wagging the staff back and forth, back and forth. Jesus begins his walk across the field and is soon approaching the lad.

"Hello!" Jesus calls. "I come in peace. My name is Jesus, and I travel alone."

As Jesus draws closer, he can see the boy is around eleven or twelve years old and stands confidently in the face of this stranger. The lad is dressed modestly in a short woven shirt tied about the waist with a multicolored band. The garment hangs to midthigh. Beautifully crafted leather sandals wrap around each calf muscle and tie just under the knee. Atop the boy's head is wrapped a multicolored shawl, tied in the back. Along with the shepherd staff, the boy carries a sling that hangs from his belt, just as Jesus does.

Jesus thinks this must be a bedouin lad based on the colors in the clothing. He smiles broadly as he closes the distance to within a few feet. Jesus extends his open hands toward the boy. In return, the boy says in perfect Aramaic, "Hello, Jesus, my name is Ebber, and I attend my father Jonna's flocks. How do you come to be here in the wilderness of Edom?"

"I have come by way of Ashod, that city of the Philistines near the coast of the Great Sea," Jesus offers.

Ebber picks right up on that and says, "Ashod huh? I have heard many stories of that city and its people. I think one day I would like to travel there."

Jesus looks him in the eye and says emphatically, "Nothing good comes from Ashod! You would be best served by staying far away from that place!" Continuing, Jesus offers, "I only went there to find some friends and see for myself the degradation and perversion that has overtaken the city. Indeed, it is far worse than is told. I have traveled many miles since leaving my home in Nazareth and shall travel many more before my Father, YHWH, sees fit for my earthly mission to begin. I travel doing His will and listen to His leading for the people I come in contact with. My travels thus far have been mostly in the wilderness to the north and east of the Hebrew nation."

Young Ebber is now very curious about this Hebrew man before him and says, "You say you are a traveler, a man of the wilderness? My father has told many stories of a Hebrew prophet from the north that performs miracles and healings and intercessions in the lives of those he meets. This man too is a wanderer, such as we are." Ebber pauses. "Do you know of this man?"

The smile on Jesus's face tells Ebber he has found the very wanderer, and Jesus affirms this with, "Truly, you have discovered the man of whom your father has spoken. My Heavenly Father has given me a vision and mission for this earth and its people. I simply serve the Most High and wait for my time of revelation."

"Really! It is you?!" Ebber asks excitedly. "You surely must come and stay with us! My father will not believe this! He will be here tomorrow morning to check on me and the flock, but we can go right now to find him!"

Jesus laughs and says, "I would not expect you to leave your flock and go for your father now. If you don't mind, I would welcome the chance to stay with you for the afternoon and evening and learn more of the shepherd's calling and responsibilities. Perhaps, we can learn something from each other."

Ebber thought that was a wonderful idea and said so. These two strangers sit as different as night and day yet now joined in mind and spirit for this moment, this minute, these hours in time. Here sits Jesus, the Son of Man, filled with all the knowledge of the universe that was and is yet to come. Also sits this shepherd boy Ebber, a common lad by most description in age and knowledge. They sit as equals on this day, looking at each other's lives with wonder and amazement.

Jesus smiles as he listens to Ebber relate his relationship with the flock.

"I provide for them daily. They cannot survive without me. Therefore, they listen to my commands and heed my call. They know my voice. If one is lost, I secure the others and seek the lost until they are found. I lead them to known springs of life-sustaining water. I lead them to graze in green pastures. I stand guard over them in the darkness and protect them from lions and wolves and bears. I would lay down my life to guard theirs. From time to time, I must use my shepherd's staff to bring them back in line. My father trusts me to keep them all."

Jesus is astounded and humbled by the depth of understanding in this boy's description! Jesus also realizes that this young shepherd boy has just summarized the reason for his own earthly existence! "Thank You, Father, for providing this wisdom from the heart of a shepherd boy! Amen!" Jesus whispers.

As Jesus sits and listens, he remembers accounts of another shepherd boy written about in the scriptures. That boy would one day be a mighty king. King David, of whom Jesus's very own lineage can be traced. It is no accident that these accounts and memories are now living in Jesus's presence with this bedouin boy.

As Ebber finishes his own insightful description, he excitedly defers to Jesus. "If you could now please tell of your travels and the people you have met, and of course your life as a prophet, healer, and miracle worker! Please!"

The laugh of Jesus paves the way for the stories that follow. And once again, Jesus tells of the night time revelations from YHWH. He tells of his tutelage at the knee of Mary and Joseph and the prophet, Eli. He tells of encounters with beasts and robbers and demons and dead men. He relates visions and dreams, healings and miracles. Of earth past, present, and yet to come. And sadly, the corruption and slavery of the human spirit that abounds in the darkness that is Ashod.

Ebber sits wide-eyed and engrossed in this illuminating conversation. Wonder of wonders! Jesus has revealed himself more fully to this wandering shepherd boy than he has to any other. And yet he does not feel exposed or compromised in any way. This too is part of the Father's plan.

This time of sharing has cost them the entire afternoon. But neither would have it any other way. Jesus and Ebber sit as equals and now also as confidantes. Each knows about the other, but they also have learned more of themselves. The evening is suddenly upon this strange mix of age and occupation. The camp fire is aglow and a ground squirrel is cooking over the flames. The squirrel is the result of Ebber's great aim. Small talk now fills the conversation as they wait for dinner to be roasted.

Soon they share the meal. Jesus asks how far south Ebber and his family have traveled, and he responds, "We have been all the way to the Red Sea and have touched the mountain called Sinai. But as is the nature of our family, we never inhabit a land but constantly are moving."

Jesus offers, "It is certainly a wonderful opportunity for you to see other peoples and lands. I think that I too will head to the south and see the lands spoken of by my ancestors." This conversation has helped make up Jesus's mind.

"Ebber, you are a wonderful part of my journeys and discovery. My heart's only desire is that you and your family would one day come to know the fullness of YHWH's love for you. When you hear of my death, do not be discouraged as you certainly will hear of my resurrection also. Believe it!"

Jesus continues, "The night air is cool, and the moon's glow speaks to me. My time with you is coming to a close, and my Father urges me south. I will travel by the stars tonight and bid you good-bye."

The shepherd boy and the Savior embrace like long lost friends. Then Jesus fades away into the night. And so it is that Jesus, once again, becomes the purposeful wanderer. His mission for this moment is to explore, meet, and learn. He must continue to fill his bag of human experience with everything that can be touched, seen, and heard. His time is drawing near to the beginning of his ordained ministry.

Jesus knows this swing south through the lands of the forefathers and times past will end soon enough. The voice of the one calling in the wilderness is already being heard to the north, and providence warrants their meeting shortly. But then again, that is another chapter in Jesus's life, the last chapter.

The coming days and nights and months will be filled with awe, wonder, and intercession. Jesus will dip his toes in the Red Sea and climb the heights of Mount Sinai. He will walk the trading routes of King Solomon and think of the gold and silver for the temple that came that way. He marvels at the copper-and-iron smelting pits at Ezion-geber. He will trod upon the soil of the Edomites and Moabites and think of King David and his conquests. His prayers on Mount Sinai will mingle with the early prophets such as Moses and Elijah. Jesus will sip the bitter water of Marah.

He recalls the provision of manna and quail for his people during the Exodus from Egypt. He marvels to find the western shore marker at the exit site of the Red Sea crossing erected by Solomon so that none would forget. And of course, Jesus is humbled to think he has pressed the ground where Moses received the Law. What amazing opportunities and insights have come his way, and Jesus thanks the Father continually.

He has experienced all this world has to offer and been guided and protected by his heavenly calling. He has tasted of feast and famine, want and plenty, life and death, joy and sadness, sight and darkness, love and hatred. Jesus has witnessed the depths of human depravity and seen the heights of human love and devotion.

Jesus has now completed his time alone. He will straightway be required to apply his life lessons and divinity to the benefit of those who will heed the call, His call. He turns northward once again and envisions his travel back through the wilderness of Paran and the plains of the Negev. Perhaps, he will return by way of Petra or Kadesh Barnea. Whatever path he travels, he knows where he is headed—back to Nazareth, back to see his mother Mary, back home.

And so it is that Jesus's travels of discovery are completed. And in a sense, he has traveled full circle. What is contained within that circle that is now his human life, is all that is important. He has experienced everything this earth has to offer and completely understands human existence. Jesus's earthly understanding mingles with divine reason and firmly rests upon his shoulders in Nazareth. It is from here, Nazareth, that he truly will begin his calling and fulfill his destiny.

Last Road, Last Hurrah

Cris and Daani both sensed the finality in the good-bye with Jesus. They have their whole adult life ahead of them, and they are not about to throw it away traipsing around the wilderness with Jesus! They purposefully enter back through the east gate and wonder what has transpired since they were momentarily distracted.

Back to the business at hand! They are sure that Sheba will have some choice words for them when they return. They certainly are not looking forward to that. A small price to pay, they think. Soon, all memory of Jesus and his visit are gone. Their lives are back to "normal," and the world revolves around their activities and relationship with Sheba. Just like they want it.

As the days and months and years accumulate, they grow deeper in debt and owe more to Sheba. She controls their very existence, and they don't even see it. Even if they did, they wouldn't care. Cris and Daani are in the very seat of power in Ashod. Their entire teenage and adult life has been spent within the shadows of the walls of the temple and the city. They are very, very comfortable here.

One day, as they sit at Ben's doing everything and nothing, their destiny comes knocking and catches them napping. Ben sides up to them and nods, saying, "Daani, Cris, good day. There is a traveler at the door that has asked for you two by name. Do you wish to speak with him?"

Cris answers curtly, "Who is it, and what do they want?"

Ben continues, "I don't know who it is, but he says he has word for you from your hometown of Bethlehem." They never get word from Bethlehem. Just as they never send word home. Daani sits up and says, "Send him over right away!"

They sit in anticipation of the messenger from Bethlehem, and soon see a lone man younger than them by a couple of years. He winds his way through the tables and patrons. He heads directly to their table. Neither Cris or Daani move to stand and remain seated. Daani fidgets with the handle of the sword in his belt, looking in the face of this stranger.

"Greetings, brothers!" the young man calls on his approach.

"Humph," Cris breathes, "we certainly are not your brothers! Why have you interrupted us, man from Bethlehem?"

"Indeed, Cris, you *are* my brother! I am the youngest son of our father, Samuel and our mother Ellise. I bring news from Bethlehem!" With that, both Cris and Daani sit up and take notice.

Cris stands and embraces this man, a stranger no more. "No way! Sit, brother, sit!" Cris exclaims as he grabs a chair from another table and drags it over to theirs. "That would make you my brother Seth! Right? Man, I haven't seen you since we left Bethlehem all those years ago! You have really grown up!"

Seth smiles broadly to think that Cris would remember him! And sits. "Ben! Ben!" Cris shouts and waves, "Bring more drink and bread!"

"So good to see you. What brings you to Ashod? We haven't seen or heard from anyone for years!"

Seth looks at Cris and begins, "Well, we really had no idea where you even were for years. After you two took off, we thought maybe you were killed or joined a traveling caravan or something. Then after a while, we began hearing of two Jewish men in Ashod that matched your description and soon found that indeed, it was you and Daani. We have really heard some far-fetched stories about you two," Seth says, trailing off.

Cris pipes in with, "You do know you can't believe everything you hear. So what else is going on in Bethlehem?"

Seth continues, "Another thing that might interest you is this. You remember that big guy Cain that took you to court and all that stuff way back when? He was found murdered not too long after you two left Bethlehem. That was many years ago, I know. But it looked like he was jumped and robbed and got his head smashed in."

Daani and Cris look at each other with a start. It has been many years since they even have thought about that incident. They had agreed to never speak of that day again, and here it was being mentioned. It was indeed a memory they would rather not have.

Daani says, "No kidding. Too bad about that." And quickly changes the subject. "So, Seth, what really brings you to Ashod. Why are you here?"

"Well," Seth begins, "when you guys left, it really hurt the families a lot. Daani, your mom Naomi really took it hard and became very sick. We took her in to live with us to be a part of our family. That seemed to do wonders for her health, and Naomi has become my second mom. She is great, Daani, and has never forgotten you. She misses you so much!" Seth pauses. "Naomi is the reason I have travelled to Ashod to find you. Daani, she needs you real bad! She is very sick again, and we do not know how long she will live."

Seth looks directly into Daani's face and says. "Daani, her only wish is to see you before she dies! This is what she prays for day and night! I am here to plead with you to come back to Bethlehem to see your mother!" Seth stops, and a tear runs down his cheek, dangling from his chin. He wipes it off with the back of his hand and eyes them both. Daani and Cris seem unmoved.

The years of living life constantly staring at the broken and hopeless lives of others have made them calloused on the outside. Daani's stomach is twisted like a pretzel, and Cris's heart is doing flip-flops. Neither show their true emotion as dutiful soldiers of darkness.

The silence seems to last an eternity. The brothers-in-arms wordlessly mull their options. It comes as no surprise when they reach a conclusion silently yet in unison. Cris voices their agreement, "We must speak with Sheba and let her know what has happened. You can wait here at Ben's, and we'll come back shortly." Cris gets up and motions for Ben to come over.

Ben arrives at the table, and Cris says to him, "This is my brother Seth. Get him whatever he wants. We'll be back in a bit." And with that, Cris and Daani exit the inn, leaving Seth under Ben's care for the moment. They leave the inn and head directly to the temple.

Daani says as they walk, "I don't know about you, but I think it is time we make the trek back home. You know our parents aren't getting any younger, and it has been many, many years since we have been outside these walls for any length of time."

Cris says, "You are right, but you are also forgetting one small detail. We have to get this past Sheba, and that won't be an easy thing!"

"Right you are!" Daani concludes.

Their arrival at the temple was no different than the hundreds of other times. They enter through the main archway and motion for a guard to come over. Cris says, "Tell Sheba we need to speak with her in private, as soon as possible."

The guard nods affirmatively and says over his shoulder, "I'll see if I can find her," and walks away in no hurry. The duo prop themselves against a column inside the archway and begin watching the steady stream of people coming and going. Those entering carry some object for an offering or sacrifice. Those leaving are empty-handed.

Soon, they see Sheba emerge from the back and motion for them to come over to her. She smiles as she waves to them. Sheba stands expectantly, looking at these two young men walk purposefully toward her. She admires her handiwork in these two. Neat, clean, and handsome—they certainly are men to be reckoned with. All thanks to her guidance and teaching and, of course, her perverse influence. Job well done!

"What is it, boys? I didn't call for you today," Sheba queries.

Daani says, "Can we sit somewhere out of the hustle? We need to talk with you."

"Sure, sure. Let's go over to the south room. It'll be nice and quiet there." Sheba leads the way around the outside of the main auditorium to the room.

Inside, they find a couple of benches and piles of furs and linen with pillows stacked beside. Sheba reclines on the floor on the furs, and Cris and Daani sit on the benches across from her. Sheba looks wonderful as usual.

Daani begins the talk, "We have just received word from Bethlehem. My mother, Naomi, is very sick, on her death bed."

"Yeah," Cris continues. "My brother Seth showed up today with the news. He says she won't last long at all."

Daani offers, "I really would like to go and see her, and Cris should come. He needs to see his parents and family too. It's been so many years since we've been back home."

"Well," Sheba curtly responds, "I don't see how that concerns me, us in any way. You know I can't afford to have you leave me! I need you by my side! I might need you for something, an emergency!" Sheba's agitation begins to show. "Besides, Ashod is your home now! You owe your allegiance to me! Not your dying mother!"

She stands to her feet with her hands on her hips and hovers over her slaves. "Have I not been your mother! Your provider! Your lover! Have I not given you everything you always needed and wanted?" She is seething now! "And you want to leave me and return 'home'? How dare you!"

Daani and Cris have shrunken noticeably under the vicious barrage and wince at every word that is spit from her mouth. They do not cower, but they don't look up either. Cris finally looks up and into the fiery glare of Sheba, "Look, Sheba, this is something we really need to do. Besides, we'll only be gone for a couple of days."

"We'll be right back!" Daani nods in agreement at these words.

Sheba remains standing and screams her response, "Did you not hear anything I have said? You cannot and will not go! Is that clear enough for you?" Her tirade is interrupted for a moment by a knock on the wall from outside the room. Sheba storms to the doorway and screams out, "What? We are busy here!"

A temple guard sheepishly retreats from the doorway calling over his shoulder, "Sorry, just making sure you are okay!" It is obvious now that the sound of Sheba's voice has carried from the confines of the room. This makes Sheba even more incensed! She whirls to face the boys who are now standing.

Cris leads the way to the door with Daani following close behind. They approach Sheba with a resolve refined from years on the streets willing to do whatever it takes to protect each other, and right now, that means standing up to Sheba.

Cris stops just short of the doorway, facing the fuming siren. He purposely states, "Sheba, we have been your faithful servants for the past fifteen years. We have never asked you for anything we have not earned. Now you must listen to me."

Sheba does not let Cris say another word as she cuts in, "I must listen to you? No, you have it all wrong. You! Do! My bidding! That is all! The day that becomes too hard for you to understand is the day that you are no longer welcome or needed here!"

Daani has stayed quiet for long enough and calmly offers, "This is a simple request. The world will not stop if we visit our aging and dying parents! I for one am going. We sought only to inform you of our leaving!"

With that, Daani pushes past Cris out the door and into the temple proper. He does not stop or wait for Cris. He knows Cris will have a very hard go of it with Sheba and can't stand to watch the climax. Daani heads through the main archway to the outside steps. He stops just before reaching the top step, takes a deep breath, and stands motionless.

Cris looks long and hard at Sheba. For the first time in his life, he sees something he doesn't like about her. The love he has carried for this woman since the beginning is clouded, and his heart is torn. He looks with steely determination at Sheba and says quietly, "Sheba, it is you who must make a choice now, not us. We are leaving for a while to return to Bethlehem. You must now decide how you will handle this situation."

Cris's calmness has not moved Sheba one bit, and she gets right in his face. "It is obvious that you two have made up your own minds! Against my wishes! You may not like what this decision of yours will cost you! No one goes against my wishes!"

With that, she slaps Cris hard across his face! He doesn't even flinch. The sharpness of the slap sets his determination in stone, which in turn crushes what is left of his love for Sheba. He whirls and marches out the door, leaving Sheba alone in the darkness.

As he heads toward the temple archway, Cris reaches up to feel his stinging cheek. He fights back the tear forming in the corner of his eye. He sees Daani standing on the portico, his back to the temple. "Well, brother," Cris says as he approaches, "we are on our own now. Just you and me like the old days." Daani looks up and nods in acknowledgement.

He doesn't have to say any more about it. The finality is marked with a red handprint on Cris's cheek. "Let's go get our stuff and hit the road," Daani says. "The sooner, the better for me." They swing by Ben's to pick up Seth and stop at their place to gather clothes, travel gear, and money. They quickly leave the confines of Ashod spurred on by an unseen push that neither recognize as their own destiny.

No sooner than they clear the east gate of Ashod and take their first step toward Bethlehem was Sheba at work against them. The most high priestess and overlord of Ashod wastes no time calling together her underlings. This meeting will expose Cris and Daani and their unforgivable sin of disobedience. It has set the stage for judgment.

Sheba calls in every favor she has to exact her toll. There is glee in her dark soul as she plots and embellishes the charges against the sinners. The two that once were her darlings will now feel the sting of her talons. She has already given them up for dead.

It is determined. She will send a runner to Bethlehem to tell the governing authorities there that Cris and Daani are thieves and have stolen from the temple and her. They are not to be taken lightly and are armed and dangerous. They should be arrested but use caution in the approach.

She also sends messengers to Jerusalem and into Galilee with the same death warrant. She knows what this means for Cris and Daani and shows no remorse in her resolve. Sheba will not have their blood on her hands directly—another perfect plan.

Satisfied her scheme is solid and set in motion, Sheba dismisses the meeting. As the chief temple guard begins to leave, she calls him over and says, "Go and find that good-looking young Hebrew. I think his name is Saul. Bring him in to me."

"Yes, madam," answers the guard as he trudges off.

Sheba smiles and says to herself, "I think I just may have a position for him!"

Death in Bethlehem

Daani, Cris, and Seth waste no time putting distance between themselves and Ashod. They are determined to see Bethlehem as soon as possible. They can rest when they reach the village, and for now, they push on through the night. The next morning finds them about ten miles from reaching Bethlehem. They stop for food and drink and rest.

Cris and Daani finally have the chance to notice their surroundings and take a breath. "It sure feels good to be out of that big city," starts Daani.

"Yeah, I never realized how much I miss being out in the wild again," says Cris.

Seth pipes in and says, "I'll tell you something else. I never thought a city could be that big and so stinky!" They all three laughed at that observation.

Soon enough, they were back on the road and striding toward Bethlehem. They really had no idea what they would find upon their arrival. But right now, anything was better than what was behind.

By midday, they could see the walls of Bethlehem. Picking up their pace in anticipation, they smile at the memories. They waste no time heading across town for Cris's house. The streets seemed vaguely familiar and somewhat welcoming especially compared to the last time they had traveled them.

Soon, the willow tree in front of the house appears more inviting than ever and much larger than before. As the trio approaches, they could see numerous people gathered beneath the trees branches, sheltered from the overhead sun. A woman in the shade looks up at their approach and waves at Seth, the only one she recognizes. Others soon were looking that way, and each began rising from their seats. Ellise, the woman who had waved, breaks from the shade runs to the three.

She heads directly into the embrace of Cris, who consciously returns the hug. "Cris, my son! Even you have returned home! Praise be!" cries Ellise. Turning to Daani, she says, "Look at you Daani! Your mother will be so glad to see you! Our sons who were once lost have now returned! Come, come. There are people you must meet and see!" Ellise grabs Cris and Daani by the arms and marches them to the willow tree.

Seth follows close behind. His task is now completed. The chatter immediately intensifies as the back slapping and hugs are let out. In the midst of the greetings, Daani steals away and heads inside the house. He has only one on his mind now, and that is Naomi, his mother.

The dimness in the interior quickly vanishes as his eyes adjust. There in the corner is a bed tucked neatly to the back in the main room. A lone figure lays propped up on one elbow, looking toward the doorway. Daani can see the form quivering from where he stands and calls out, "Naomi, mother, it is me, Daani!"

"Of course, it is you, Daani!" Naomi whispers in a strained, raspy voice. "I just knew you would come home! Now come closer so I may touch you and see for myself!" Daani does not readily recognize this feeble voice, but his heart says run!

And he does. Falling on his knees next to this frail woman, he gently rests his head upon her stomach. Naomi places both her trembling hands on his head and weeps. No words are spoken as once again their spirits unite in silent accord, renewed in the moment.

Daani feels the tremors that pass through the once strong hands. He too weeps. "Mother," he cries as he lifts his head, "I have missed you so, and now, once again, we are together."

"It is well, son, that you have come home. YHWH has seen fit to prepare me for the end. You were the only thing that has kept me here—His promise to me of your return."

"And now He has kept His promise," Naomi's frail voice trails off and vanishes in a sigh. Daani holds her close.

His head rests upon her breast as he searches for a beat or breath—anything. He whispers to the Almighty, "It is I that have forsaken my mother and You, my God. Forgive me and welcome her home."

Daani covers his mother with the bed clothes and rises from her side. He slowly walks to the front doorway and stands beneath the frame. In view of the entire family, he reaches up to his collar and tears the cloth from neck to chest, falling upon his hands and knees.

Instantly, the wails of the women fill the air, and mourning begins. The finality of Naomi's passing hits the entire family hard, very hard.

Since Cris and Daani's departure from Bethlehem, Naomi had been invited into Ellise and Samuel's home. Her street life was over. She had become a very important part of the family and a second mother to the children. A constant source of joy and help for Ellise, Naomi had really fit in.

Her absence will have an immediate impact on the family. The following days and weeks of mourning brought family and friends together and gave Daani and Cris the opportunity to get caught up on news and local events. They were settling into the laid back life of a small Jewish town and were beginning to like it again.

It is in this vein that they are brought up to speed on Jesus also. They learn of his latest and greatest exploits. The tales are unbelievable. And so is the fact that Jesus now has a "following" and disciples. People flock to hear him speak. There is even talk of Jesus being the long-awaited Messiah sent by God Almighty to redeem His people. All the miracles and signs point to this truth and Jesus himself has made these claims!

Cris and Daani talk long and hard about these things. They have run and played and laughed and cried with Jesus. They have known since the very beginning that there was something special about him—guarded and protected, wise and perfect, divine.

Betrayal Fulfilled

The time of mourning has passed. Cris and Daani have been moping around Bethlehem for a couple of weeks. The entire town now knew that they were back, and the stories from Ashod were on everyone's lips. Most people would look and point or gossip when they walked by. They took it all in stride and minded their own business.

It was just another one of those days as they sat beneath the willow tree. The morning had run its course, and the midday sun slowed everything down. As they talked quietly, they were approached by two officials who seemed purposeful as they advanced. The boys were kind of surprised when they walked right up to them.

"Good day, Cris and Daani," the tall one said, nodding to both at the address. "We have received a message from Ashod for you both. If you will come with us, we have it at the town hall."

Cris looks up, squinting into the sun and says, "A message huh?" Looking at Daani, he winks and says, "Well, I wonder who that could be from!" He gets to his feet and says, "Lead the way!"

They fall in behind the officials and walk toward the center of town. "You don't suppose that Sheba has had a change of heart about us, do you?" Daani says, smiling.

Cris laughingly says, "You didn't think she could run that city without us, did you?" They are in great spirits as the town hall looms before them.

They follow the two men inside and walk toward the opposite wall. As they near the long table in the rear, they hear shuffling behind and notice two soldiers fill the space in the doorway they had just passed through. As the two officials circle behind the table, two more soldiers enter the room, one from the left and one from the right.

Cris and Daani are both on alert now, and they noticeably stiffen as they stop in front of the table. "So where is this message that you have for us from Ashod?" Cris says as he grasps the front edge of the table before him. Daani instinctively turns slightly to his right with his back to Cris sizing up that soldier.

The tall official edges back from the table a bit and clears his throat before speaking. "We do have a message from Ashod, but it is about you two. It seems that you have been accused of crimes against a woman there and against the temple of Dagon. Since you are Hebrew, we have been ordered to turn you over to the authorities in Jerusalem. There you will be formally charged and put on trial."

"These soldiers have been sent to accompany you to Jerusalem," that said, the officials begin to move away from the back of the table, but Cris interrupts their retreat.

Banging his fists down hard on the table, he shouts, "By whose authority are these charges leveled?"

"That is not our concern. The message is official and so you must face the charges! For the sake of your families, please do not make this any harder than it already is!" The town official is visibly shaking now and just wishes to be out of this situation.

At the last exchange, the soldiers have advanced a couple of steps forward. Cris has turned from the table and now stands next to Daani shoulder to shoulder. Daani has placed his hand on the butt of his sword, and Cris sizes up their position.

They have no doubt they could better the soldiers, but they also consider that one or both of them may be injured in a fight.

Both parties are coiled for each other to flinch and then Daani remembers a similar situation they were in many years before. *Funny,* he thinks as their youthful standoff with the lion just outside of town comes to mind.

A smile crosses his face, and he relaxes his muscles standing straight again. Cris senses the break, and he too stands tall. They will live to fight again, so they think. But of course, YHWH has already numbered their steps, and their final path now stretches before them.

That path leads to Jerusalem and a reunion of sorts. They have for-gotten the promise they made to themselves many years before. As they sat in the jail cell in Bethlehem as teens, they swore they would never leave their fate in the hands of others again. But that was a long time ago. They are taken to Jerusalem. The trumped up charges are upheld. The sentence is handed down without delay. A scourging will precede death by crucifixion.

The Truth Revealed

Jesus travels south from Nazareth to meet John the Baptist on the banks of the Jordan River northeast of Jerusalem. The Holy Spirit descends. He spends forty days in the desert being tempted. The baptizer is arrested, and Jesus heads back north into Galilee.

Jesus calls Simon, Andrew, James, and John as disciples, the first four of the twelve. Jesus's entire earthly life has pointed to this beginning. He is well prepared and seeks only the Father's will. He embraces his calling with his very life. From the beginning of his ministry, Jesus is under the dissecting eye of the authorities. Religious and governing officials alike watched with disdain, this Jew that would feed and heal and mingle with the multitudes and gentiles. At first, they were content to let this charade continue, and they scoffed at the stories told. But then, the people began having faith and believed and called for this man to be their Messiah! This now begins to undermine the established system.

The movement swells and threatens the very foundations of government and the established religious society. Action is taken. The band of followers is quickly rounded up and then dispersed.

Jesus is forsaken by one of his own and arrested. The trial finds him guilty and sentenced to death upon a cross. Beaten, torn and condemned is the leader, this Jesus, the Christ. The movement as well is defeated and headed for a footnote in the annals of history.

And so it would have been if it were not for the cross and the plan set forth by the government of heaven before the beginning of time. Jesus will find His true fulfillment today. And it will come at the crack of a whip, the clanging of hammers, and the point of a soldier's spear.

Between Heaven and Earth

The tears of his beloved mother stain the parched, sandy ground near the hole for the base of Jesus's cross. Mary's wail is heard over the wind that whistles along the hilltop. It nearly covers the sounds of the falling hammers. Nearly.

Hammers that sometimes ring in unison as the three are spiked tight against the wooden beams. The three are strong this day, and none cry out. Their voices have been stolen by the scourging that has left them drained, weak, and bloodied.

Each cross with its occupant secured is raised, slowly at first as the lifters gather themselves. Then with a burst of strength and speed, the men heave!

The base finds the hole! The swift drop of the upright cross stops with a loud thud! The surrounding ground vibrates as the cross settles in. Jesus is beyond the feeling of pain now. His cross has been raised first and still sways as the guards set the wedges to keep it straight. From the corner of his vision, he sees movement and then a thud to his left. And then another thud to his right.

Vibrations travel through the ground and up the center cross—Jesus's cross. Two other crosses have finished their set. Jesus twists his head to see the men who have accompanied him on the hill today. Through blood-streaked vision, Jesus glimpses the two. Both lifted to die upon a cross. Their builds are familiar—one broad and muscular, one thin and lean. One wears dark blood-streaked hair and the other copper-colored blood-streaked hair. Both are torn and bloodied nearly beyond recognition from the whippings.

From Here to Eternity

All three have been given a reprise of sorts after the crosses take a set. This is done so the spectators are provided ample time to watch and note the agony and suffering of the men and their families. The officials use these public displays of justice as much to discourage illegal behavior as to display the latest killing techniques and, of course, to show their power over the masses.

This will be an all-day event. The pain seems to subside, replaced by numbness. The body has become numb enough that the other senses begin creeping back. In between the wailing and weeping, Jesus hears the insults hurled in his direction from the crowd.

"He saved others but himself he cannot save."

"Save yourself, O Chosen One of God!"

"Son of God, save yourself!"

"How pitiful, just pitiful!"

"King of the Jews? Ha!"

These were the very same people who had followed him from village to village and coast to hilltop a few days before. They had gladly accepted his teachings and food and miracles. And they now spat insults his way. The agony in his heart overshadows the pain of his flesh. And then a nearer voice, one to his left, pierces the other sounds. It comes from the same level as Jesus's head, cross-bar high.

In tune with the venom from the crowd, it yowls, "Aren't you the Christ? The Savior? Save yourself and us! Can you?"

Then to Jesus's right, another suspended voice cries out, admonishing the howl from the left. "Don't you fear, God? We deserve the punishment we are given as payment for our deeds. But Jesus has done nothing wrong! Jesus! Remember me when you come into your kingdom!"

A smile forms and cracks the crusted blood upon the lips of Jesus. And Jesus replies, "It is true, my brother. Even today, you will be with me in paradise."

Jesus is glad in his heart. "One is saved. None need despair. But only one, so all prepare." The day on the hill of Golgotha is far from over.

The coarse ropes tied around the arms of all three men make them stand upright with backs pressed tight against the roughhewn wooden beams. Shortly, the crucifixion guards will see that the crucified men are still too strong, too alive. They will remove the ropes holding them upright. The crucified will then have to support their entire weight on the spikes driven through their ankles and wrists.

The pain will be too much to bear, and they will begin sagging, pulling against the spikes. The weight of their own bodies will cause them to suffocate slowly. If their leg strength is still great enough to support their body and breathing, their legs will be broken by a swing of a great wooden headed mallet, a bone-crushing blow.

The ropes are loosed. Two stand tall, and their legs are broken. Three sag against the spikes. The suffocation begins. All three die.

The One is pierced through the side needlessly. Blood and water cascade from the wound. It runs down His side and dampens the groin cloth. It races down His thigh and reaches the knee. It flows down His calf and mingles with the blood drawn by the spike at the ankles. It covers His toes.

And then the blood droplet takes shape. It can cling no longer to the whole. It falls. One drop and then another. Each unfettered and free for an instant before hitting the earth. They dampen the dry, thirsty ground.

Darkness rejoices and blankets the earth. Heaven gasps and catches its breath. The three crosses are laid back. They rest upon the earth. The guards wrench the spikes from the wrists and ankles. The families rush in to recover the bodies for burial. Mary stumbles to the center cross. Undone by what she has just witnessed.

Ellise and Samuel attend to the left cross. Other family members and friends attend to the right cross. Even as Mary presses her ear against the still cold chest of her beloved son, Jesus. She hears something! Not breath, nor heartbeat but the burgeoning of heaven's divine seed!

Death cannot take hold. Heaven exhales in victory!

Characters in Order of Appearance

- Mary—mother of Jesus, wife of Joseph
- Joseph—earthly father of Jesus, stone mason by trade
- Jesus—the Christ child, heaven-sent, born to Mary and Joseph
- Naomi—mother of Daani
- Daani—son of Naomi, Jesus's boyhood friend
- Ellise—mother of Cris
- Cris—son of Ellise, Jesus's boyhood friend
- young girl in alley, victim of Cain
- Cain—murderer, rapist, father of Daani
- Samuel—father of Cris
- Jonah—Bethlehem town elder, one of three law givers
- Eli—prophet of old, returned to earth to mentor Jesus
- Benaiah/Ben—innkeeper in Ashod
- Sheba—siren of Ashod, high priestess of Temple of Dagon
- Caleb, Ruth, Marai, and Simon—family of desert travelers
- Alli—temple of Ashod patron
- Daughters of Alli—stolen as payment to Dagon
- Thieves in the desert—Jesus's harsh judgment applied
- Adah, Levi, and three little girls—fisherman's family living on the sea coast
- Adar—twin sister of Adah, living in Ashod
- bloodied man—patron of Dagon
- Ebber—shepherd boy
- Seth—Cris's brother

About the Author

Born and raised in Monroe, Michigan, Chip graduated from Jefferson High School and Monroe County Community College. He attended Grand Valley State College and graduated from Eastern Michigan University with his BS and MA in Education. Recently retired from teaching at Huron High School in New Boston, Michigan, Chip resides with his wife Judy in Monroe. They have two daughters and four grandchildren and enjoy the many activities their extended family offers.

Chip is actively involved with his church and its many outreach ministries and serves on the deacon board. He has been a lifelong reader, and *Left Cross, Right Cross* is his first novel.

Chip is currently working on two other writing projects one being a spin-off of a character from *Left Cross, Right Cross* and an interesting work on Scripture from the viewpoint of the archangels.

CPSIA information can be obtained
at www.ICGtesting.com
Printed in the USA
FFOW03n0323210518
46725023-48851FF